D0486049

Yvonne Vera
Butterfly Burning

Yvonne Vera, one of Zimbabwe's best-known writers, was born in 1964 in Bulawayo where she now works as the director of the National Gallery. She is the author of several books, including the novel *Under the Tongue,* which received the 1997 Commonwealth Writers Prize (Africa Region).

BUTTERFLY
BURNING

BUTTERFLY
BURNING

Yvonne Vera

FARRAR, STRAUS AND GIROUX
NEW YORK

Farrar, Straus and Giroux
18 West 18th Street, New York 10011

Printed in the United States of America
Designed by Lisa Stokes
First published in 1998 by Baobab Books, Zimbabwe
First published in the United States by Farrar, Straus and Giroux
First edition, 2000
19 21 23 24 22 20 18
Library of Congress Cataloging-in-Publication Data
Vera, Yvonne.
    Butterfly burning / Yvonne Vera.— 1st ed.
      p. cm.
    ISBN-13: 978-0-374-29186-0
    ISBN-10: 0-374-29186-1
    1. Young women—Fiction. 2. Zimbabwe—Fiction.   I. Title.

PR9390.9.V47 B88 2000
823'.914—dc21

                                        00-028834

To Terry Ranger

I could speak until tomorrow
of a glorious friendship and faith

BUTTERFLY

BURNING

one

There is a pause. An expectation.

They play a refrain on handmade guitars; lovers with tender shoulders and strong fists and cold embraces. Birds coo from slanting asbestos roofs. Butterflies break from disused Raleigh bicycle bells.

In the air is the sound of a sickle cutting grass along the roadside where black men bend their backs in the sun and hum a tune, and fume, and lullaby. They are clad in torn white shorts, short sleeves, with naked soles. The grass burns over their palms where they reach over and pull at it, then curve over the sickle and beyond, pull, inward, and edge the grass forward with the left palm. They bend it toward the left shoulder and away from the eyes. Sweat drips like honey over the firm length of the arms tearing and tugging and splitting the grass. Often they manage to pull the roots out of the ground; to free something; to conquer a stubbornness; to see what is below; to touch what keeps something alive and visible. Sharp rays of the sun drop along the sharp curve, and flow along the rotating glint of the silver sickle. The arm agile, the arm quick over the grass.

The tall grass sweeps across the length of their curved bodies, above their bowed shoulders, and throws a cascade of already dry seeds over their bare arms. The grass is a thin slippery tarnish as it waves smoothly. It sways away and again away in this current of heated air. There are seeds, light and flat, like tiny baked insects. Falling down, with their surfaces rough, flat. They waft into the thickness of grass.

Each motion of the arms, eyes, of the entire body is patiently guided. The palms are bleeding with the liquid from freshly squeezed grass. The brow is perpetually furrowed, constricted against this action, and against another, remembered; against regret for a possible inaction, and against each memory that dares not be understood. A silence, perhaps, or something near and anticipated but not yet done. There is waiting.

Their supple but unwilling arms turn, loop, and merge with the shiny tassels of the golden grass whose stems are still green, like newborn things, and held firmly to the earth. The movement of their arms is like weaving, as their arms thread through each thicket, and withdraw. This careful motion is patterned like a dance spreading out, each sequence rises like hope enacted and set free. Freed, stroke after stroke, holding briskly, and then a final whisper of release. The grass falls. Arm and arm and arm of it. It falls near and close to each curled body. The grass submits to the feet of the workers who step over it to arrive where the grass is high and stands defiant. They hug it indifferently, concerned only to keep its tassels from their eyes, spreading it away. With an easy ease they escape the fine flutter of dry seeds raining downward. The men cut and pull. Cut and pull. They bend, cut, and pull. It is necessary to sing.

They cut and level the grass till the sun is a crusty and golden distance away and throws cool rays over their worn arms, and the sky dims, and everything is quiet except the spray of light breaking and darting between the grass tossing back and forth above their foreheads and above their eyes now filled with fatigue. The grass is swishing hopelessly below the shoulder, under the armpit, grazing the elbow, and its sound folds into a faint melody which dims with the slow dying of the sun, and each handful of grass becomes a violent silhouette: a stubborn shadow grasped.

The men twist the grass together and roll it into a large mass, stacks of it, and gather it into heavy mounds to be carried away the following day. Their bare soles grate against the stubble now dotting the ground, raised like needles, and where the grass is completely dried, turning to fierce thorns. The men, adapted to challenges more debilitating than these, discover welcoming crevices, empty patches where the grass has been completely uprooted and the soil turned to its cooler side. So they place their soles to safety, their heels to a mild earth. The work is not their own: it is summoned. The time is not theirs: it is seized. The ordeal is their own. They work again and again, and in unguarded moments of hunger and surprise, they mistake their fate for fortune.

As for healing, they have music, its curing harmony as sudden as it is sustained. It is swinging like heavy fruit on a low and loose branch, the fruit touching ground with every movement of the wind: they call it Kwela. It is a searing musical moment, swinging in and away, loud and small, lively, living. Within this music, they soar higher than clouds; sink deeper than stones in water. When the branch finally breaks and the fruit cracks its shell, the taste of the fruit is divine.

This is Kwela. Embracing choices that are already decided. Deciding which circumstance has been omitted and which set free, which one claimed, which one marked, branded, and owned. The beauty of eyelids closing; a hand closing; and a memory collapsing. Kwela means to climb into the waiting police Jeeps. This word alone has been fully adapted to do marvelous things. It can carry so much more than a word should be asked to carry; rejection, distaste, surrender, envy. And full desire.

Trust lovers to nurture hope till it festers. Always wounded by something—a word, a hope, a possibility. After all, they are the kind of people to get caught by barbed-wire fences. A part of them calcifies, dries, and falls off without anyone noticing or raising alarm.

Bulawayo is this kind of city and inside is Makokoba Township where Kwela seeks strand after strand of each harsh illusion and makes it new. Sidojiwe E2, the longest street in Makokoba, is fresh with all kinds of desperate wounds. Bulawayo, only fifty years old, has nothing to offer but surprise; being alive is a consolation.

Bulawayo is not a city for idleness. The idea is to live within the cracks. Unnoticed and unnoticeable, offering every service but with the capacity to vanish when the task required is accomplished. So the black people learn how to move through the city with speed and due attention, to bow their heads down and slide past walls, to walk without making the shadow more pronounced than the body or the body clearer than the shadow. It means leaning against some masking reality—they lean on walls, on lies, on music. One can always be swallowed by a song.

The people walk in the city without encroaching on the pavements from which they are banned. It is difficult, but they manage to crawl to their destination hidden by umbrellas and sun hats which are handed down to them for exactly this purpose, or which they discover, abandoned, at bus stations.

They understand something about limits and the desire that this builds in the body. Their bodies long for flight, not surrender, simply the need to leap over the limit quickly and smoothly without bringing attention to oneself. This they do, often and well.

After all, they are the ones who keep the pavements clean and sweep the entire city. They have the duty by virtue of their own humility and obedience to pick up the white men fallen on the pavements while the door swings open, once more, from the smoke-filled taverns, and voices are heard briefly before the door swings back in. They help these men into an upright and respectable position, then lead them into solid black cars. Then they spit on the pavements and move on.

When they arrive back in Makokoba, Sidojiwe E2 is flooded with Kwela music. The feet feeling free. Hostilities too burdensome to give up. There is a search in the narrow gutters for passions and separations. The people smoke burned-out stubs and tone their fingernails with nicotine, and lovers mourn with joyful release. We do it together. This and that—fight, escape, surrender. The distinctions always unclear, the boundaries perpetually widening. Kwela music brings a symphony of understanding, then within that, other desperate confusions. Poverty prevails over innocence. In such times, a song is a respite.

Dying in your sleep. Not once, but several times. Fleeing from an image reflected from translucent shop windows. And then, again, sleep. Afterward, a brief resolve not to bend. Then saying yes.

Kwela strips you naked. Anything that reminds of pride can be forgotten in the emptiness introduced. A claim abandoned. A lover lost. It is the body addressed in its least of possible heights. A stone thrust. The knees down and the baton falls across the neck and shoulders. Kwela. Climb on. Move. Turn or twist or . . . move. No pause is allowed, and no expectation of grace. Kwela. Cut, pull, bend. It is necessary to sing.

Then one chaotic evening the word is pulled back from the police Jeep by whoever is listening in sleep as a car tire digs along Sidojiwe E2.

It is freedom and style and survival with no fear of flight or stagnation. This is the city and the pulse of possessing desire. Something that can be recovered, must be restored. Even if it may now be frayed or torn. It has to be put back somewhere where there could be a hint of belonging fastened on somebody. If not freedom then rhythm.

Patience is abandoned and something else witnessed: a raised eyelid; a handshake; fingers snapping. Then slow courtship under the tall trees which divide the houses from the red roofs of the police camps. These trees have been brought from faraway lands. They are the sort of trees which do not seem to need water, or when they do, send tentacles that burrow deep, no matter how hard the ground. With no regard whatsoever for the lack of pliable soil, or absent drops of edible rain.

Underneath these trees, the lovers stand forlorn in the cluster of large silver-and-white peelings which are curled among the thin pointed leaves now fallen, where forked roots break the earth. The dead leaves cling to their tinge of green, resisting their separation from the tree. A shell expands, dries. Pods explode and spread black rounded seeds to the ground. The seeds have hard surfaces, with gray veins.

So tall, these trees, firm and impossible. They look as though they have been built by hand to carry improper histories. A strong scent rises from the base of the tree, from the roots perhaps, like a fading dream. A beautiful, precious, remembered scent. Wafting and vanishing like a mist. The trees make the search for love good by their strong presence and brief odor. In the night—moonshine, words, a happy tune, fate, and distance are shared. The lovers bask in immaculate dreams. Kwela includes the harmonies one can name, and misname. There is night.

Kwela in daylight is incessantly bold. No parting or other phenomenon of rupture. Some fighting. A slap and a slash and more Kwela. Torn leather shoes rubbing against cement. Tar melting in the hot sun as though newly spread. The sanitary lane carries the secrecy and stench which envelopes the waste of every character—wasted time, wasted love, wasted this and that.

Time flips like a tossed coin and in the luster and swinging surprise it is nothing on a single day to hear a thief leap over hedges on Sidojiwe E2 and by noon to listen to bicycle bells in the city center. There copper coins crash and jingle onto the pavement as they are swept out in the early hours of the morning from empty city taverns which have NO BLACKS signs, WHITES ONLY signs, and CLOSED signs which say OPEN on the flip side signs and dangle CLOSED from ornate door handles, and outside . . .

There is music.

t w o

The voices of drowned men cannot be heard.

The drowned die in whispers. They die in infinite solitude. The air leaves their bodies in a liquid breeze. First they sink as far as the weight of their bodies will allow, then they float. They touch the surface with their faces, not their arms, with their lips. Nothing will bring them back. Their skin is lighter than air. They can see even though all their senses have been silenced. They are not blind. Their gift is to see through every particle of water. They breathe in water. They seek flight, lighter than raindrops. A body floats to shore. Everything grows heavy, is buried, decays, or dries then burns into a silver ash of wood.

The men are left up in the tree all day and night. The moon gives them a living light that rises like a soft layer of smoke from their bodies, a spiraling mist in which their skin melts off. The tree itself is veiled, then its strong branches emerge, denying secrecy, and reveal the broken figures weighing down upon their arms. The branches bend down. High up off the ground, some lower. Seventeen male bodies blown into the branches by a ruthless wind.

Night. Mist ascends like luxurious tears and claims the men. They are swimmers, in the mist pulling up and then down the tree, like floating wood. Swimmers with no arms. Floating and forever dipping down. Sinking in a tree which has become a lake of light. Eyes not closed, not there, cavities where a child might store a pebble. Palms touch, tucked flat between their thighs.

The dead men remain in the tree for days. Their legs tied together, their hands hanging close to their stomachs. Toes are turned down to the ground as though the body would leap to safety. The foot curls like a fist, facing down. The feet of dancers who have left the ground. Caught. Surprised by something in the air which they thought free. The limbs smooth and taut, of dancers in a song with no words spoken. A dance denied. A blossom in a wind. A dark elegy.

Morning beams a sharp daylight that cuts a sudden profile of their human form. The sun breaks behind each shoulder. The rope is no longer visible. The men are standing in the air with their heads looking downward. The dead men are living, no longer floating, standing motionless and upright, with flickering flame on their bowed faces, foreheads, and forever broken necks. Naked shoulders quiet and mute, the entire body too stiff for awakening. The earth too still. The dead as dead; the living equally dying and bewildered.

In the morning they absorb the joyful light, which is full of pods breaking, releasing a multitude of white fluffy seeds which float toward the dead and glow like night insects. They float across their still shoulders and fall into the river. The pod explodes quietly, like a mind dying.

They are not men, but shadows. They are silhouettes. The men remain there till the ropes holding them up are weakened by decaying flesh, and succumb like all things softened and decayed; or is it that the neck has softened before the rope, and the dead bodies swoop down and lie unheeded?

The birds fall down with the bodies.

It is not a place with large trees. This tree, like these deaths, is a surprise. Away from the Umguza River which sings a lullaby each morning whatever the season, there are no trees. It is a river because it has a bed along which its water runs. In the dry season, the low water makes a whirring sound over its rocks. The ground so hungry that the slightest rain makes the grass spring from the earth.

Beyond the top of this singular tree, beyond the Umguza River, the women raise their voices at dawn to mourn seventeen men and thousands more. Their resistance to the settlers has been silenced. They weep but nothing can be heard of their weeping. In the night, amid bursting fires they listen to the pounding of the hearts of their men. They are not allowed to touch the bodies. They do not grieve. It is better that the murdered are not returned to the living: the living are not dead. The women keep the most vital details of their men buried in their mouths. They receive lightning from the sky with their bare hands and with it, they rename each of their children; the living and unborn. They find new names for the dead and utter them in daylight. Then everything changes; everything is new. The men are buried in their mouths.

The women had watched from below the wide tree whose branches were high off the ground. The men were empty with nothing in their hands, nothing in the arms, nothing on their bodies except large marks from the constricting chains in which they had arrived. They had waited under the shade of the tree in a straight row, their legs steady in spite of the chains, their eyes clear and peaceful. They were placed safely under the shade as though they needed one last comfort. Above them, empty ropes hung, endless circles of heavy and solid rope, seventeen circles in all, dangling down, and seventeen naked men on the ground. Waiting, in circles.

Life is drained out of the scalp. Life is pulled out of the body like a root. When a man falls free from the tree and still breathes the knot is slowly released. He is pulled once more off the ground and yanked back into the branches. A man can be hanged more than once. The first, he watches himself die. He dies several times. Then something crushes in the roof of his head, his faith a wisp of flame thinner than life. Only a perfect circle can hang a man. Then death is sudden and quick. Before death, there is silence. The body is undone by a violent touch. A rope. These are prisoners in a tree.

Death is as intimate as love. Fumbatha thinks of his father, who is one of the seventeen dead, a shadow in which he constantly searches. April 1896. Fumbatha was born the same year in which his father was hanged. Fumbatha—this is how a child is born, with fingers tight over an invisible truth. This is when birth is least different from death— where death and birth touch; like the shape of a wing and the invisible air in which it moves. A child is born with a unique secret however concealed. Fumbatha, his small hand open and spread on the lap of his mother. She delivers words that are arrows. His palms burn as though covered with wounds which have been rubbed with salt till he wants to close them. He closes them. Trapped in his fingers are the words his mother has given him. A single seed gives birth to seventeen more, to a thousand more.

When he is fourteen years old, she wakes him in the early morning and walks with him across the Umguza River. The river winds forward over the rocks and thorn bushes. Not too far away, they can see the smoke encroach from the city center and hear, in this early morning, the clamor, the urgency of trains. Throughout their long walk she says nothing. Finally, she stands with him under a large tree which he has not seen before and calls, "Fumbatha . . ." Her voice is a whisper. Fumbatha is not sure whether he should answer her or if she is addressing someone else not there, a memory in her hands. "Fumbatha . . ." She is searching the air with her voice and walks round the tree. He is not sure if he should follow or remain still till she has found the secret buried in the roots of that tree. She has been here before, without him. When she calls again, her voice is impatient and he knows that she had expected him to remain close to her, to witness the shiver of her arms, to see her eyes burn. His birth a witness to dying, a pledge to life. She expects him to know his link with the past.

His father died on the tree. Fumbatha looks everywhere. There is no sign of death. His mother continues to whisper his own name in the quiet wind. Fumbatha is not the name of his father. He wants to know the name of his father. He cannot ask for the name of a dead man. He dares not intrude. Only the dead can receive his name and be free. His father has vanished. A liquid that has sunk into the ground.

In sleep Fumbatha drowns in the deaths of the seventeen men. Each night, he listens to a cloud descending from the sky and pulling the bodies apart till their spirits are rent from their bodies. The birds feed on the dead but free them from an eternal silence. The men borrow voices from the birds and speak in fluent sounds. Clouds gather in the sky and there is heavy rain. Umguza is in flood full to the brim. Children drown because they understand nothing of rivers which are in flood and step into the water as though it were a glittering layer of stone, and when the water does not resist, their timid feet are charmed. They leap in and their bodies race down the river like wood. Water swirls round the trunk of the tree on which the men have died. There is nothing we can do to save the dead. If they wake, whose life would make them whole again?

Fumbatha wakes in the night to the sound of a van speeding past Sidojiwe E2. A prisoner. His father a stranger.

Nineteen forty-six, like all time before him, waits.

three

Sidojiwe E2: the children sit on empty, rusted metal drums and talk of cars passing along Jukwa Road, a street of tarmac which stretches longer than they can see. They find rainbows.

They hold their eyes against the tight brightness of the sun reflected on metal and read the number plates on the cars with awe, constantly astonished by the sight of white men with lingering gazes and hasty waves. Waving at them with hesitant limbs.

The children wave back, reluctantly, and hasten to polish bottle tops held between tiny thumb and forefinger till all the ink is gone from it and a pure silver emerges under their nails. The children use small and dangerous pieces of broken glass to scrape the ink off; in between, they consider the cars coming toward them, between the thumb and forefinger.

They blow the red and blue paint flakes from their hands. Some of it remains stubbornly pasted and they wipe these bits off, carelessly, against their rough and worn clothing.

They blow rapid and warm breath across empty bottles. The bottles whistle. If a strong wind approaches the children run into the middle of Sidojiwe E2 and hold the bottles flat on their palms and raise them up in the direction of the wind. Then they stand aside, flat against the barbed-wire fences. The music tears from the bottles in brief and surprising interludes. Their combined effort uncovers a tolerable melody. Often the experiment yields nothing. It is faithfully repeated.

There is a choice of guitars made out of empty, battered cases of Olivine Cooking Oil. And flutes. Of pawpaw stems. The white juice, running down to the lips when the flute is held up, has to be tolerated. It dries gradually. The taste makes the lips burn.

Next, they pick the skeleton of a broken old umbrella and hold it up to the sun as though they have found shelter of a separate and distinguished kind. They huddle under the umbrella and pretend heavy rain is falling and that their tattered clothes are now wet. They bend over, drenched, and wipe water seeping down their foreheads, and draw their dripping arms under their chests to retain whatever warmth they can, in this beating rain. One of them holds the handle of the umbrella upright. The children raise their eyes to the empty sky: it hardly ever rains.

Cars, carrying inquiring stares from their drivers, continue to break the silence and banish the bruising rain. The drivers threaten the children by moving off the road toward the abandoned drums, swerving, swearing, skidding. Wheels squeeze the air empty of hope. Someone screams, hidden by a cloud of mounting dust. The tar is a narrow strip, the edges a cover of dust.

The children laugh and race beneath the overturned large metal drums and hide in the darkness and warmth inside the place where they have put treasures no one can envy or claim. An echo, laughter, as the children dangle their arms on imaginary car windows, and stagger and stare, whistle and beckon. Their eyes glazed with liquor as real as the beating rain. They too examine misfortune.

Hidden in their closeness the children hold their pulsing hands together. Shoulders touch. Toes scratch the folded rim of metal. Naked feet are sealed against every humiliation, held carefully under the body. Knees are folded. Elbows bend and burn with the powdery rust of the metal which peels into thin crumbling flakes, like dead skin. The children touch again and again, back to back, hand to elbow. Their lips are dry. Their voices splinter like dead branches.

The girls wait in tattered skirts which waver over their thin thighs, their breasts are flat like the bottle tops. Whispers are shared in the secrecy of their hiding place, and as the wheels outside stop and move on, inside, filled with an intuitive fear, the children wait. A sound gathers like broken glass, like bottle tops falling into an empty metal jar. They are afraid and anticipate that every disadvantage will overtake them. Whatever is not known must be without shape and therefore above every reality they have already witnessed.

Squelching wheels. Thin incoherent voices move toward them like smoke from damp wood. Perhaps something might intrude with a claim too difficult to ignore. The children see rainbows and are assured of their own kind of permanence, so they hold their breath and cover their voices with cupped hands, and fingernails stained with rust. Coiled like caterpillars in this dark and temporary retreat, they touch every visiting belief with an anxious curiosity—and in their own unarticulated manner begin to question the whole notion of an innocent belonging. They are not free.

Inside the shelter of rusted metal are true treasures which provide relief. In these abandoned drums which have seen both rain and sunshine, a broken record rests, its sides chipped, and its black surface plastered with dust. The paper label is torn. The delicate thin lines on it are fascinating to the children, who pick a piece of grass and take turns to trace, carefully and steadily, each concentric ring round and round till the tiniest one ripples toward the middle where a large opening waits, and where two whole fingers can be inserted, and the record swung over and over in suspension. It turns dutifully till the label is blurred and none of the letters shows. And a dent forms along the fingers. The record found floating in the ditch or somewhere about is a necessary diversion.

An empty box of matches. A single leather shoe with laces still attached. A small hand slides inside the shoe and it is warm within the moist cavity—and the darkness inside the shoe can be felt with the fingers like cotton. An ink stand says London. A magnificent metal spoon with a dove embossed on it. Selborne Hotel is written along the broken handle of a ceramic pot.

The children possess nothing except an excited value placed on anything shared, and a glorious love of intimacy. They only have to look at each other to feel that they have been born not only for a healthy but for a joyful purpose, because immediately they fling their treasures into the dark corners of their hiding place and break into the day with echoes of sunlight, rainbows curling around their knees, a glory too furious and complete for adults to understand, with dreams too stunning.

There is fear in the wonder but that is rare, and they forget each negative incident as swiftly as it occurs, mumble an incoherent summary to each other, a solution, against intrusions uncharitable and alien. The children delay their next outburst only briefly before they flood into Sidojiwe E2 calling to one another as though each of their voices herald a unique awakening, then they fall like dropped leaves beyond the ditches, the pungent and decayed water. They weave their own ceaseless talk of imagined places.

When you are a child, floating is the very essence of living, and flight too. Each offers a type of vanishing. The body is without weight. It is a liquid without form except that of the vessel it chooses to inhabit—therefore it is shaped like air, becomes intangible. It flows translucent, absorbing all color and sound. Poised and perfect like a single drop of water.

Along Sidojiwe E2 is a long ditch which carries waste from the factory on the other side of Jukwa Road. This ditch is black with sediment, a viscous factory water and oil, harsh yet fascinating to young minds and absolutely tolerable to their senses, going past and flowing, over the other side of Makokoba, pouring into the Umguza River. The children do not wander that far, not beyond the boundary where the houses stop suddenly then yield to rock, to distances of flowering thorn bushes, then further down, land so empty and barren the soil simply slides and falls among a few stunted shrubs, scarcely living. Their houses are much closer together than the bushes, though equally stark.

The children like to remain close to the ditch, close to their own curiosity which leads them step by step to the edge of every capricious reality. After all, their own homes are not too distant from this, from that, and always, they can smell this, and that, and squalor of every kind. There are other pains.

Bicycle tire, zinc sheets, a car door. Oil breaks the light on the surface of the water in the ditch, stagnant and breeding—a swarm of insects hums incessantly like a hostile cloud. A tree grows and hangs low over the water, reflected unmoving as a thick distorted shadow with no leaves. The water trickling with oil is colorful and shiny like new fabric.

In the distance, a large tank. So large that the children along Sidojiwe E2 could all drown in it at once. The tank is full of oil. It must be filled with rainbows too. Oil and rainbows. The water in the ditch, and the oil, emanate from it.

The older children walk as far as the border which encloses the factory and touch the barbed fence. They place their fingers within the diamond mesh and gaze at the men working underneath the large tank which is raised from the ground. The men are under the tank.

Then they vanish. They vanish in a cloud of violent and impeccable flame.

Sidojiwe E2 sees the fire blaze the sky as the oil tank bursts at the factory site and the men working underneath are swallowed in the blistering flames. The children abandon all thought of their play and watch through the fences; they have seen the fire first and imagine that a special ceremony is being enacted for their benefit. They neither run away nor make a sound, instead their fingers tighten along the diamond mesh of the fence and they hold on as the explosion beats against their bodies and threatens to turn them to ash, they can feel the warm air pushing against them like a current, the fires glaze the sky like a dream, billowing with dark fuming smoke which builds a mountain in the sky, thick and blocking the sun for as long as they stand there, and in an instant they are separated from something vital, some memory which has engrossed them before this, some harmless activity, some child-nurtured desire about the unfolding of time. They tighten their grip. If they let go they would tumble into an unknown abyss. Then they press their heated faces against the wire and let it burn their faces while they stand still and smell the air perfumed with the acrid smoke which spreads sideways and upward like something living, with a will playful and bright unlike their own, an energy beyond any they can predict, they can touch the smoke because the flames are warm on their fingers, just like sun rays dropping down, and in the center of this incredible mountain the flames lick the sky like a liquid, a giant flower blossoming in the sky, its petals red and widening and spilling over the mountaintop to flow steadily out but vanishing suddenly back into the terrifying dense smoke. A solid flame. It is easy for the children to forget the men who had been working under the tank. They had watched them being swallowed by the loud rumbling, the explosion which banished every thought, and this figure rising before them is more commanding, much more rare to their curiosity, than the tiny bodies which they had watched from a distance. No one knows what judgment has brought this death, this miraculous vanishing of the living. The flames linger for an entire day till the children turn their heads away filled with ordinary desires, like hunger, and retreat into Sidojiwe E2 where they close their eyes and rest.

Afterward, they see the men rising in the ditches, like rainbows.

four

Fumbatha rests beneath the debris and rubble. He is lying on his back with the empty khaki bags of cement for a pillow, and a small gray blanket under his body. Sleep creeps up his body like a stream. He feels heavy, not just tired. The smell of cement has the effect of pulling him down and pinning him to the ground. The shovel is beside him, the ax, the bricks, the rising dust, the arid sky above. And night comes like a thief, with a gentleness that caresses the eyes with gleaming broken rays which disappear into the horizon like sparks of flame into a lake, and then a shadow falls, and night, and then a sudden downpour of stars. The intense heat of the afternoon is forgotten; there is the cold coming in like an embrace in the velvet blanket of night. When the night becomes too cold, he might creep under the lorry and the safety of its large wheels. Perhaps pull a plastic bag and cover his body with it. He might even move over the half-built wall and fold himself into a corner of the emerging room. He will whistle a tune till it dies on his lips, with sleep. He will sleep in a tune.

He sleeps near the Umguza River which rises like a whip and breaks out of the earth to flow smoothly through the rocks. A full river on this dry earth where the sun is seen rising before it rises, before it has any rays, a pure circle without any light and it seems possible to touch it. There is nothing else but this river and this harsh light and earth, the ground is a smooth floor dipping down into a seamless horizon. So the river is something to look at, to marvel, and live near. Just a short distance from it, the land is nothing but bushes blooming with large thorns that jut out like porcupine quills, the thorn on each bush is thick like branches, with the tips sharp and pointed, tight, holding on to the last drop of water inside them, seeking the water not in them, and way beyond, the cactus bloom within the broken rocks covered in yellow moss, and within the cracks are thin gliding insects which look like chipped sticks, like pieces of broken dry grass which have been eaten away by ants. On the other side of the river, the city is a commotion of activity. The city has swallowed the river.

Fumbatha watches the sun rise in the river, his own reflection in it. He sees the glare grow and spread on the surface of the river before he lifts his eyes up to the sky. This is morning. The sun is in the river till it finds its way out and sweeps into the sky where it belongs, sliding sideways till it climbs out and disappears from the river into the bank, and the water glistens, shimmers with the slanting rays.

Where it can the river digs ancient histories out of the ground. A piece of old broken clay. A necklace made of glass. Bracelets with markings telling of birth, marriage, death. A hidden message. An invitation, tempting and undisclosed. Fumbatha retrieves a bracelet and wears it on his right wrist. It is cold over his body and the water is still dripping from it. He washes it clean till it shines. A bracelet, a chain. Broken memory and a buried touch. He encloses it, encircles it by placing his left thumb and forefinger over it, touching time like something solid which can be born several times before it dies. A healing fragment, a wish. Time can be passed on like a gift held in the hand. He will give the bracelet to Phephelaphi when he returns to Sidojiwe E2; a piece of time. Anything can vanish but time. It leaves evidence of everything it consumes.

Too little survives the intrusion, the trains, the buildings blocking every pathway, the labor of the hands. At the back of Fumbatha's every dream is a sorrowful wind blowing like a hurricane. A buried song builds out of the ground like a whirlwind. The village where his mother raised him is no longer there. Fumbatha knows too little of the world of his father except that others fought on the side of the white men. Even then, there was that sort of self-betrayal and mistaken courage: identity had already become a curious detail to living. One side won. It is the nature of victory to measure triumph in the silence or death of the other.

There is the pressure of survival, and money is needed for shelter. For almost twenty years Fumbatha has done nothing but build, and through this contact, Bulawayo is a city he understands closely, which he has held brick by brick, on his palm, felt the tension of effort over his back. He has held this city, without a clear emotion of anger or love; with an unresolved abandon. He has watched each building acquire its own mood, the darkening walls where the factory smoke has tarnished the paint, where the train smoke has built over the front building of the main railway station. He has built. When he is dead, his hands will remain everywhere. He does not know if he is part of the larger harm. He does not understand it at all except the lingering hurt which needs not to be understood to be felt. Sometimes the present is so changed that the past is linked to the present only by a fragile word. To build something new, you must be prepared to destroy the past.

An ancient bracelet; a new lover. He met Phephelaphi on the Umguza River in 1946 on an afternoon that followed a morning such as this, golden with noon rays edged like knives which hit the surface of the river and left the water rippling, the water tossing gently wayward over the beaten bedrock. Since then, whenever he sees the sun near the river he knows it has sprung out of the water into the sky; it has risen from the river.

He had been sitting along the river for half the morning in the worst heat of the year, and it was nearly noon, his feet naked, and if he bent his toes down he could dip them in the water and feel it move swiftly past in warm waves. The rock he sat on was half submerged in the water. She emerged breathless and gasping for air beneath his feet and rose out of the river like a spirit. The water streamed down her face, sparkling rivulets. She wore a thin cloth which clung over her like skin. She placed her hands above the rock where it leaned into the water and dragged herself out.

Nothing bothered her, the wet hair, and the water which continued dripping down her back as they spoke. It was the brightest morning for Fumbatha, her eyes glittering like jewels before him, her arms the same color as the rock on which she rested. Each of her motions carefully guided, and her voice rising drop by drop, toward him, smooth like the water before them. She was sunlight. Her beauty was more than this, not expressed in her appearance alone but in the strength that shone beneath each word, each motion of her body. It was as though she made a claim with each movement, each word spoken, but none of this was a burden to her, it was just how she was. What she had become in her growth. Phephelaphi was unaware of the manner in which she had, by her presence, transformed him. They were strangers.

They had already met. She had swum toward him from the opposite shore, hidden under the water. She could see him all the way from beneath the water. She rose out of the water like the sun and he looked at her in total surprise. The words tumbled out of her as she spoke and gasped for air. She was water and air.

She had come to the Umguza River to swim.

"Is it not true this is the only river here?" she asked with a wild agility that he envied and knew belonged exclusively to the young. She insisted that it was important to know how to swim, even if there was only one river, not much rain, and therefore very little chance to drown.

"It is the only river," Fumbatha agreed. "This river grows among thorns. This river does not belong to dry land. It is greedy and gives nothing of its water."

She stood up. His world changed.

"If you move that way"—he pointed in the opposite direction to which the river flowed—"you will meet this same river. It is the same river many times. You will meet it if you walk straight on in four opposite directions."

"Then this is not dry land. There are many more rivers than I thought," she laughed.

She dived back into the water before he could say anything else. She was gone only briefly. But time had stood still with her arrival. Had he imagined her presence and their entire conversation? She was an antelope. No. She was a being entirely from the water even though she reminded him of an antelope. The river was not as greedy as he had said. It had given him this woman, spitting her onto the rock like a dream. He waited. Fearful that he would wake and find her gone.

"Where do you live?" he asked, unsure if he had the right to ask at all. Her courage to be here on her own enabled his question and ease.

He asked as though to protect her. He wanted to protect her; it was impossible they had met only to part again.

"I used to live on Jukwa Road in Makokoba. My mother died. Her name was Getrude. I live with Zandile, a woman who was very close to my mother for many years. We live together on L Road, which is not too far from Jukwa. I have only been living there for a few months since I lost my mother."

Fumbatha lowered his eyes. She did not hesitate in her response. Instead, she sat on the rock beside him and lay down. The rock was warm. She placed one arm over her forehead and shielded her eyes. He glanced at her through the corner of his eye. The water was caught in her eyebrows. When he asked for her name, she half rose from the rock and looked at him in disbelief.

"You already know where I live and that my mother Getrude died. You must ask for my name first, before you ask about where I live. But I will tell you because a name is not a secret. My name is Phephelaphi . . ."

Something had already happened between them. She looked at him intently to see if telling her name meant something, if it changed anything about their meeting. The Umguza continued to cast its crystal waters past their feet and sweep on to the next bend. He listened. He had never heard this name before. He looked at her carefully as though seeking in her something more familiar which he could believe in and make their meeting true.

"Phephelaphi?" he asked. He held the name closely, on his palm. It was like holding one part of her inner self. He never wanted to let her go, even though they were strangers. He could never free her, even if she rose and disappeared once more into the water. He would remember her. He would hold her. Fumbatha had never wanted to possess anything before, except the land. He wanted her like the land beneath his feet from which birth had severed him. Perhaps if he had not been born the land would still belong to him. The death of his father had not heralded birth.

Fumbatha had never met a woman who helped him forget each of his footsteps on this ground which he longed for. Here was a woman who made him notice that his feet were not on solid ground but on rapid and flowing water, and that this was a delight, that there was no harm. It had been enough for him to work as he did, to live as he did. When he was with one of the many women in Makokoba, Fumbatha knew how to soothe both their imagined hurts. His attachment ended there. In the morning he woke with the same puzzled stare. They swapped names and each said one true thing. It was a necessary but final exchange. As she closed the door behind her and moved on, the woman held the true thing close to her and she was able to walk steadily down the street even though a voice told her this true thing was a burden and best forgotten. Fumbatha knew those women from Makokoba so mighty in their pursuits, to whom truth was so rare they treasured, recognized, and pried it instantly even from strangers. He forgot the woman quicker than he forgot her name, except, perhaps, the one true thing she had whispered.

To find shelter. Here was a woman who made Fumbatha finally relax his palms and look high up into the sky. He was no longer on guard. Here was life and water and shelter of a kind. He could not argue with her shimmering presence. She gave him faith. Without her saying anything he felt she had offered him a promise. Fumbatha was eager to begin. With her arrival he discovered a desperate fear large and unnamable which he could not abandon. It was he who needed refuge.

"My mother named me Phephelaphi because she did not know where to seek refuge when I was born. She slept anywhere. She had no food in her stomach, but her child had to sleep under some shelter. She had hard times. As soon as I was born her struggles began. When I was born, she had given me another name. She called me Sakhile. Then she discovered that Makokoba had no time for a woman who was raising a child on her own, so she renamed me. I was six years old by then. She still called me Sakhile, but she sat down often with me and said that Phephelaphi was the name she had now found for both of us. She had struggled."

When Fumbatha continued to look confused Phephelaphi offered a solution.

· "You could give me another name. I do not mind being named by a stranger. I do not mind being renamed if it makes the present clearer." She laughed.

Fumbatha was not certain whether she was happy or sad. He was so used to the chameleon quality that women had with names. A woman could offer a name as a pronouncement of her contempt. Not necessarily of this particular man, but to deal with a solid pain from yesterday, and if she was looking to the future, the name confirmed her suspicion of betrayal, revealed her entire struggle with time. She could wear a name easily like a dress and each moment you looked at her she was checking how well the name fit, if it hid well her wounds, but mostly, if the name showed the smooth sway of her limbs. Sometimes a woman forgot her own mistruth, and cursed, and asked you to stop calling her that name she knew nothing about, that awkward name which you had both heard spoken at the same time. She insisted that this surrender was the only true thing she could give; she offered her true name like the most harmless temptation there is. Then a man knew that he had reached her genuine self and that she wanted a taste of something true, not some disguise scalding her hips. Fumbatha examined Phephelaphi closely and tried to forget whatever he knew about the women he had met in Makokoba.

They had long ceased to be strangers.

There was an open road between them. In that short time, something bound them—the young girl, to the older man. He hesitated, because she was so much younger. He felt wearied by the loss he already anticipated, by the memory of her which he already treasured. What could she know about a man who loved the water falling from her arms. What could she love about him. What could she give to him without loss to herself. Without perishing beneath the stream. What words would he use to hold her and keep her still. An older man with his ankle held in a river. Who was he. Would she pause long enough to hear him say her name again?

He watched as she threw herself into the water. She stayed under for such a long time that he thought she had drowned. She returned to the surface and said it was important to stop breathing for as long you could. It was even more important than to survive.

"I feel like a thief," she said. "Everything I own I have stolen. The time I spent with my mother was something I had taken. It was not a gift. I stole everything, then time, and event, stole the rest that had been given."

She moved away from him, back into the water.

It was not hard, after seeing her several times after that, for them to decide to live together on Sidojiwe E2. Phephelaphi had finished school. She had no relatives. Her mother Getrude was dead. When the decision was shared with her Zandile was relieved to watch Phephelaphi pack her suitcase and carry it onto her head and leave the one-room house they had shared only briefly. Her relief was so clear that Phephelaphi refused to let Zandile accompany her to Fumbatha's house. She refused too the skirt which Zandile insisted on giving her to keep.

Zandile said the skirt was the first clothing she ever bought when she arrived in the city those many years back, and she had kept it because it was her only link with that past, and with Getrude who had witnessed her wide-eyed stare as train whistles beat toward them, and they both drifted nervously past the streetlights as they dimmed and burned out. It was a time like no other time. It was Getrude who had shown her where to live and how, who could challenge every closed door and murmur a consoling tune.

Phephelaphi looked at the skirt which carried one large pleat opening over the right knee and she let the skirt drop back into Zandile's arms where it belonged. Nothing could bring Getrude back. If she had burned her mother's dress she had no time for any other woman's priceless memories.

It was Boyidi who heaved the heavy suitcase onto Phephelaphi's head and she left. Boyidi and Zandile both watched her walk slowly down L Road, the suitcase above her head, each of her strides pronouncing a changed womanhood, till she turned into Jukwa Road where she had begun. Phephelaphi was able to see the house she had been living in before, but decided to forget what memory was there. Fumbatha waited for her on Sidojiwe E2. Nineteen forty-six was fast paced and promised a sultry escape. She liked its middle-of-the-year mood which held the bluest sky she could ever dream of. A time rich with tantalizing winds, soft but cold, which made her curl her fingers tightly around the slippery handle of the suitcase in order to warm them. Fumbatha was waiting so she walked faster.

It was he who asked, she only permitted all the questions. It was a relief for her to be with him. She felt safe in his adoration. She loved him and held him to her so that she could never sink down to where she could not rise.

Something was in her, mute, but when he was in the room, she kept all her thoughts at bay. He filled her with hope larger than memory. There was nothing she looked forward to except being with him, and each day opening like a folded petal. When he walked into the room each of her arms waited. She forgot everything and relied upon his generosity and the motion of his body toward her, on his every thought and attention.

"I am always stealing. I do not mind stealing from you," she said teasingly. He loved her because she said nothing about love. She loved him because he said everything was about love.

There was always sunlight when they were together. He longed for her deeply even while they were together. Her active laughter. Her lack of fear. She questioned everything.

"Why will they not let black men drive the trains? They know everything about the trains."

She quarreled with him even when he was quiet and had not said anything. She quarreled with herself. She argued with time. She argued with the memory of her mother. How could she have been her mother when they did not know each other's proper names. Then she told him.

Of the small room her mother had found and kept her in, of the knock on the wooden door in the middle of the night, of the certainty with which her mother rose from her bed to the door, of the intense darkness outside. She saw her mother standing with her arm resting on the other side of the doorway. A darker screen from the darkness beyond. Her mother stood like that for a long time, talking in whispers to someone on the other side. She could not see who it was, so she watched her mother, a tall erect shadow, her head touching the top of the doorway. Then she saw the arm falling slowly downward. She expected her mother to turn and move the door, to close it.

Instead, the fall of the arm was followed by the entire body. Her mother, sideways, hit the door. It was the sound of the door, the weak wood cracking with the impact of the body followed by the sound on its loosening hinges which she heard before she rose from the floor from where she was looking up at the arm now falling like a broken limb. When she went close to her mother, there was no obvious sign of harm. She was not even sure her mother was dead. Then she saw the deep hole on her chest. It seemed a long time before the blood rose to the top.

A stranger had shot her mother. For days and days after that, the arm kept falling from the doorway. This to her was now the symbol of death. Then the dress in which her mother had died was brought back to her by a white policeman. A white man had never stood so close to her. She had a really good look at him. She read nothing in his face. When he turned his back she took a candle and set light to the dress. The police were such a careful lot to remember to return the dress to her. The dress came in a bag. The bag was inscribed in red ink—Emelda.

Phephelaphi signed the bottom of a piece of paper which was held out to her. Some details were already filled in. Date of death. Cause of death. She had to fill in the name of her mother. She wrote Emelda, as it said on the bag which came with the dress. She was angry at the policeman for not knowing the proper name of her mother, and she decided not to offer him the truth. Under the dotted line where she had to put her own name, she hesitated. The policeman had not bothered to ask for her name, even when he collected her mother's body, and not even now when he brought her a dress from a woman he named Emelda. It was the same green dress her mother had worn. She wondered why her mother had been renamed.

She looked up at the firm brown cap of the white policeman and continued to hold the papers. She saw no harm in him. He looked as though he had the whole day to wait for her to decide. She wrote in her neatest handwriting—Getrude. Her mother's name was Getrude. She had adopted the name of her mother for the report, and somehow, she had separated herself from the event. Her mother placing her own name on the papers, for a woman named Emelda. Phephelaphi felt safe and handed the papers back. If she had any money and proper means her mother's death would be hers, now it belonged elsewhere. She had nothing. Still, she thought someone would come to invite her for the burial of her mother. She waited inside the house. After seven days she knew that this would not be so. Seven days is a very long time. A long time lasts less than seven days. A moment is an eternity. The worst theft leaves you barren, the best lightens your burden.

Fumbatha could no longer imagine being in a room without Phephelaphi in it. He wanted her beside him. It was easy because they only had one room, neither of them had anywhere else to go while they were at home together, in the time before evening, before morning, all day they were together. He protected her and when he watched her walk along Sidojiwe E2 on her own, he felt threatened and had to close his eyes till she walked into the room and called his name.

He had to leave her several times in order to work at different construction sites where often he was too tired to return home, or where the expense of paying for transport would have used up whatever he had earned. He had to stay away and earn something good for them. He stayed away less often. When he left her alone, he had a terrible void which made him tremble.

He opened the door wondering whether he would find her gone.

Fumbatha had no idea that one day he would open the door and find her gone, wishing he could close it again, wishing he had never left her at all; she would be in flight like a bird, laden with the magnificent grace of her wings. She would be brimming with a lonely ecstasy gathered from all the corners of her mind. She would be whispering something which he could not hear, a message he would recall much later, when all his senses were finally free: he had moved from his own song into her astonishing melody.

That would be later, occurring right in the middle of 1948, when each of their lives had yielded an eternity, and Zandile had already turned to Phephelaphi one morning and said, without scorn or truest trust, "I no longer wish to be loved, but to love. I want to find something which once belonged to me." It was a difficult search. It involved the fate and memory of everyone in Makokoba, especially Getrude, and Phephelaphi, the city itself with its nod and invitation. Including that woman Deliwe terrific in all her joys, who had all those convictions about survival, a touch so perfect it made everyone, male or female, raise their eyebrows in awe. Ultimately, it was a one-roomed love which implicated them all, and there was nothing any of them could pretend was new or painless about the situation and its ambivalent surprises.

f i v e

The music. It makes for a bargaining and temporary sort of self-love. Everyone free, the young joyful.

Zandile lets her eyelids drop, as though she has remembered something which should have been done in the morning, early, before the birds had started singing, before her laundry was hung on the hedges to dry, before she had had to drop her eyelids. Zandile has waited till the dew started melting, and the birds stopped singing, which is wrong. Noon is too much like the middle of things, not a useful time for proposals, conclusions, and disasters. Noon is just that, sunlight pouring down to melt shadows and, therefore, too many witnesses to every fall. Hurt and perplexed by the time of day which has caught her unawares, Zandile drops her eyelids and hopes that when she raises them again, not only will she be believed but the time will be way past noon.

All that Zandile intends is fighting mortality. She wants to be remembered, if for nothing else at least for her poise, her voice and liberty. So Zandile tunes her intuition to necessity and offers instant consolation. Passion is purchased. It offers many angles for escape as long as one is willing to try rising, and forever falling down.

Dazed by her own capacity for a swaying, knee-high love, Zandile folds and pins her collar down inside her dress and allows the sun to beat on her shoulders and for coy whistles to curl over her neck like a noose. Then she does what is obvious and ordinary, she raises the hem of her skirt even higher and wears high heels and hides her own tender soles from harm. Tucked safely within her low bodice are monogrammed handkerchiefs which she has retrieved from the pockets of white men. She withdraws one of them fancifully and shakes the memory of a bitter encounter off it and waves down a passing love.

Zandile beckons, recklessly. On one end of her handkerchief she lays into a neat pile the coins which she has gathered, then folds the cloth over and makes a tight knot and presses this weight firmly under her breasts. On a hot afternoon when there is no breeze or any hint of forgiveness in the air, she stands confident, in broad daylight, with one hand held to the waist and the other hand drifting slowly up and down, deeply engaged in fanning the intense heat with a monogrammed love. She lets the coins clatter sinfully to her feet.

Zandile leans languidly over her door which is split in two and holds out her arms into a half-moon, and calls out to passing loves. She wants to know where, like all the women in Makokoba, she has planted trust and why it has taken so long for it to find root. Everyone hurries past and seems not to notice or care, but she wants this vital question about her comfort heard, even if not fully answered. Zandile leans further out and whispers to passersby. Opportunity has taken too long and is buried too far in the future. She has no shape of it she can retrieve and so she feels it more useful to search through the void. First she abandons secrecy.

Her departure is tempestuous. She calls out to the firstborn sons on L Road who have names like Ndlalifa, Vusumuzi, and Bekithemba. Their mothers gaze at Zandile in amazement. It puzzles Zandile more than once where it is that women have planted trust and by what measure of patience they will be judged. She whispers louder and gives away the secrets which belong only to their offspring.

Revelations are burdensome to mere witnesses who want to hear but not to be implicated. Because Zandile insists on sharing loss she misses the entire audience and is left wondering at the quality of her own charm. She searches for a mirror and looks within it, dipping her head gently down and sideways, examining the skin powdered to an alluring brown, turning the shoulders to the side. Searching.

Looking. Zandile asks a friend to hold another long mirror to the back and searches through the mirror held to the front to see if there is anything which has been missed, something not smoothed, some dent, some sorrowful patch, but the hair at the back is a royal black and lying down pat, having been pulled straight down the scalp with a hot metal comb. Everything is where it is expected. No tear on the blouse, and the wide figure belt is observed sitting neatly, cutting along the waist. Underneath the clothing a corset does what it can to hold and keep the back straight.

No one listens. Zandile has no choice but to find calm of another kind. Handshakes cure her longing for touch and she quickly finds other means to pronounce harmony. Like all hermits she resorts to color and wears blue bangles, and lips purple like ripe granadillas. It is a time for parades.

There are invitations, raw and delicate, to be found. Zandile, with an elegant neck like polished stone stands with earrings dangling down to her shoulders, her fingers glazed with nail polish, and her lips coated with ambition. Zandile, who makes no distinction between white men and black men when it comes to pleasure and exchange, can, however, tell the difference between sunrise and sunset: at dusk, she can curl her legs around the body of a white man and listen to police whistles passing by and ambulances berate the air, curse when she sees torches brush the ceiling of the hotel room, then across the thin curtains of these rooms she watches the shadows of policemen moving past; and at dawn, she wakes in the arms of black men whom she truly loves.

There is regret under the fraying mosquito net which sweeps from the ornate ceiling and covers the swaying hips, the lifting arm, the loud mingling sigh of relief, the silence. Betrayal is mutual, distaste and curiosity an obvious and minor detail. When Zandile is done with this particular enactment, she picks some loose change from the mantelshelf and spits into the fireplace, black saliva hissing as it hits hot coal. Then she steals a cigar from an embossed gold case, clamps the lid carelessly down, and replaces this fine property on the bedside table. Carefully, she lifts her underwear from the keys of the piano, shipped from Sheffield. She stuffs the silky nylon garments into an orange handbag and slides silently out of the room and down the narrow corridors. As soon as she can she throws the stolen cigar away. Her disdain is complete.

When she sleeps with her own men Zandile stays till morning so that they can look into each other's eyes without the skin of darkness, feeling a touch of shame and sharing a lonely adult pain. She holds the single arm lying over the chest closer to her breasts, enjoying and remembering the weight of it, and rocks the man back to sleep, to wakefulness, swinging him back to a safe sleep. It is a brave and lonely togetherness. Death is far from them, though far from over, but neither is any of this about something as ordinary as giving birth. It has to do with holding the broken fingers with cracked nails between her own neat hands and bringing them delicately to her lips. She spreads the warmth of her breath like a blanket over her fingers while the man sleeps, then turns the body over and looks for scars but does not ask questions about the line of the whip digging over to the other side, under the armpit, reaching over the breast, and making a complete and fiery circle.

Instead, Zandile brings her head down to the armpit and gathers what she can of the histories of her men, murmuring something soothing and at no cost at all. At no charge. She risks only the serenity of her own mind. Close to the ribbon of seared skin she seeks the story with her eyes and lets it be, but wonders about the missing flesh, where it has fallen to and how. Further down are deep tooth marks buried behind the legs. Police dogs and chains. The ankles are blistered, the wrists embroidered with the shame of a constant struggle. If the man is lying there beside her with his flesh newly cut and swelling, then something has to be done, a bowl of warm salted water, a fresh cloth, and the wound cleaned. Desire is for the slow examining of wounds.

The year is 1945, the past flickers like an abandoned dream. No need for all that frantic touch and departure, not now. No need. Tired of this and that temporary love Zandile has long decided on Boyidi, and keeps him under her roof whatever the cost. Zandile has long abandoned the night parades, the glory of waking up in the early hours to examine the face beside her own to see what true agony she can peel off like skin off a ripe fruit and discard it, after noting carefully the core, leaf after leaf of the fruit's juicy segments, its white pith, its mouthwatering taste. It cools her memory to receive a stranger's male touch, once, twice, but she wants something else, a man to call her own. Not a stranger any more. A man with a name she can wrap around her own tongue and keep it there. So Boyidi holds her mind together, no matter how, she keeps both their fury still for in the city loyalty is a turbulent quest, not freely given.

Zandile laughs aloud as she remembers her friend Getrude, stubborn impossible Getrude who brought a baby strapped to her back to every possible appointment with every possible male stranger. What kind of mother-love was that, what kind of frenzied city-love could turn both their lunacy to good fortune?

For Zandile, each detail is now distant, secret, best forgotten.

six

There is movement.

Phephelaphi sees a man fall down, in the middle of a quarrel, in the middle of Sidojiwe E2. The man dies. Before she knows it she has run out together with the other neighbors to have a look, equally curious; on Sidojiwe E2 every absurdity is examined, challenged, then delivered to its rightful owner. The dead man's wife finally brings a wheelbarrow and carries him home, after asking the gathered people if they have never seen a dead man before. They respect her loss and keep silent. The tragedy is her exclusive property, they know, but the absurdity is not. After she has disappeared from view and hearing distance they inquire at the quality of a man who has died through the force of a word gathered in another's mouth. As far as they know he is the first man to die from such an illness.

Sidojiwe E2: Phephelaphi watches the boys released from school at noon as they scream past barbed-wire fences carrying a drowned cat. Swing it like a pendulum, and toss it onto the shoulders of the young girls. The girls scream with a fear louder than excitement. On Sidojiwe E2 you can measure fear through distance and touch; the question of immediacy attends every instance of living.

Makokoba is a place where each child has a story which stuns by its detail. Phephelaphi knows this. She sees in the children's laughter and abandon the survival of each of them, and her own. There is an eager dexterity beneath fluttering clothing. The children's clothes are torn, through time and misuse—underneath the fabric, legs, arms, faces, and voices show. In this tumbling discord, she sees the dead cat sway in its wet silky skin: black. It wavers over the split bodices and tattered sleeves.

A tall gangly boy holds the cat in a supple grip by its two hind legs. Phephelaphi peeps over the short green hedge and barbed-wire the instant she sees the boy's head swing into view behind the frenzied shrieks. On the other side, right in the middle of Sidojiwe E2, she sees the dead cat brush quickly over a short dress with no hem. A drowned cat.

An orange dress. A dress bought at Baloos Stores one New Year's Day just across the road when the shop owner has to leave suddenly and sells every item for twopence: dresses and khaki shorts, shoelaces, candy cakes, Eat One Nows, Afro combs, folded Swiss knives, Lion matches, Andrews' Liver Salts, Star Cigarettes, Golden Syrup, Minora Razors, Vanishing Pond's, Vinolia Soap, Roll-On, and Bata Tender Foots. Twopence for Tender Foots: black encasing shoes with the thick black rubber right around the edges and soft maroon soles that smelt like, well, like that.

The shop window is always closed to keep out thieves. The paraffin is precious but remains outside the front entrance, so the people feel trusted and let it alone. However, a child sometimes knocks a bottle down, or a drunken man. It makes the shop owner angry and fly into Sidojiwe E2 with his eyebrow twisted, and wave and curse and threaten the entire continent. He hovers over the now empty bottle and lets the smell of paraffin pervade him. The paraffin is swallowed by the ground. It spreads to the doorway. For weeks, Baloos Store has an identity. As though an opportunity, for flight or surrender, has been misunderstood. The paraffin trails him back into the shop. Inside he approaches his gramophone with a new zeal. His arm flying round and round and round till transmission bursts into the street. The shopkeeper knows how to reach people on Sidojiwe E2. Kwela. Aagh . . . the music of it.

It is the incident of the Red Seal Roller Meal which everyone repeats with regret, and which Phephelaphi soon shares. The shop owner does not sell the Red Seal Roller Meal: instead, he makes the people scramble over it. He throws the heavy bags from the balcony of his double-storey store which is decorated with curled, red-painted metal, shaped like lace. The bags tumble and tear from the collapse. The many arms scramble forward.

Red Seal Roller Meal. Absolutely free and no mistake at all. Finally, the flour flows unimpeded out of the bags onto the street. It rains over the waiting faces and shines like dust. For a while, covered in white flour, eager arms stretch out toward the balcony.

Then the crowd falls together and the bodies bend to the ground and find, between the ground and the wild vacancy in their hearts, the flour mixed with the soil, and with folded Fanta bottle tops, burned matchsticks, and a multitude of yellow cigarette stubs which say Peter Stuyvesant in pale white—and they gather this mass into the small metal bowls which they have brought, and examine it closely. Perhaps, between the grains of sand and the smoother grains of Red Seal Roller Meal, there was hope. They find none.

The women yank their children from the ground and proceed

home, their faces turbulent, their eyes trembling. They should have
waited in rows for the Red Seal Roller Meal, not fought over it or mis-
trusted one another. They embrace an entire loss; at least there is sharing after the event, not gloating and pride on one triumphant side. The
men, equally stunned by their own frenzied spontaneity, bow their
shoulders in resignation. The loss is shared. There is joy to destroying a
gift. On their arms is the touch of their bodies. Beneath the balcony is a
multitude of broken butterfly wings finely crushed.

The last sounds of the children vanish. The cat is thrust into the
ditch. The children disappear round the corner of the now abandoned
Baloos Store.

Sidojiwe E2. Each day, Phephelaphi grows more curious about its
lure and commands, its absent urges. How can you trust another's
hunger, another's tumult and desire: the strength of it, the force of it,
the courage not in it?

seven

One room. Solid brick walls. Asbestos and cement.

Phephelaphi and Fumbatha had a bed though it creaked and sagged and scraped down to the floor. A paraffin stove. A wire running diagonally across the room above the bed where they placed their clothing and let it hang down to partition the room; the bed was split in two, the top half on one side, the bottom on the other. The cooking was done on one side and they bent under the skirts and trousers and sat on the bottom half of the bed and held painted metal plates and ate hot meals from their laps. Two suitcases kept on this side of the bed away from the cooking space, near the small square window which faced Sido-jiwe E2. Then the entrance.

When the door opened, it hit against the metal frame of the

bed. If the bed was moved further into the room the door swung and hit the worn-out suitcases, the edges collapsed but the cover remained fastened from one side where the latch kept a rigid hold. They shoved the suitcases under the bed and only pulled them out when something urgent had to be retrieved, a letter with an old and necessary address where a request for employment had to be forwarded, or the mind simply strayed and some rummaging through the contents set life into a semblance of order. They slid the clothes to one end of the room away from the bed and suspended them high. Then they sliced meat into narrow strips and hung it on the wire. It dripped till it dried. Often, the smell of drying meat permeated the room. They opened the door wide. They placed the dried meat in plastic bags.

The walls were thin. Fumbatha and Phephelaphi were aware of the thin distance between their breathing and the next room, their thought and the next, their suppressed voices and the room not theirs, their inhalation, their motion, their surrender. They knew too that their sighs and harmonies had witnesses as bold as stars. They took note of this fact and quickly forgot it as soon as their lips touched and their thighs embraced, their fingers locked and they fell into a solitary passion, yielded to each other, kept still and close. They prayed for day to banish night, and then for night to banish day; divisions of light and darkness were tiresome, called for alterations in their habits—a door to open or close, a window to clean, a dress to be ironed, a long-lost hurt to pick from the floor like a loose nail, a knock on the door, and sunset cascading over the asbestos roofs like angry flame, and the wind blowing burned ash from dead fires into the eyes.

And, well, which was not bad at all but they did not want to remember it, the smell of roasting maize, the red glow of embers which lit the face of a woman fanning the flame with a strip of cardboard, her arms moving sideways and up, humming a tune, her lips pursed, blowing mouthfuls of cool breath onto the embers to keep the heat going and the radiance intense. From high up those tall trees towering above the houses, they hear the seeds blow and fall, patter and roll off the roofs like beads, hit down like solid rain.

They needed neither greetings nor farewells. Strictly themselves till they chose to move outdoors whatever time of day it was. They walked down Sidojiwe E2 past a cart full of tomatoes, talked to neighbors, and bought an orange and threw its peel over the barbed-wire fence. Long after midnight they pressed their bodies together and tucked into the hedges and let the patrolling police vans drive past while they fell below the glow of headlights splitting night and merged with the sound of departing wheels. They hid under the skin.

They forgot the walls thin like lace. They remembered only the shapes of teaspoons they had lost and replaced and lost again, whose every curve and shape they heaped to spilling with generous portions of either sugar or salt. That part they remembered well. A slim flat handle of a spoon which they caressed with thumb and forefinger and held gently down from sugar bowl to cup to quivering lips. The rest they did not remember. Once, perhaps, the curved spout of a teapot. They were indifferent to any other memory, especially thin walls and neighbors holding their own breath and waiting to witness what they never tired of hearing over and again, however painful, their own lonely distance reach a pitch louder than the fearless fulfilment of these two.

Phephelaphi and Fumbatha heard nothing of a neighbor's anxiety who listened through thin walls with a pounding heart. Instead, they spread the slippery sweat mounting on their own bodies and shared an intolerable tenderness. The neighbors listening not through the sheer wanting of listening but because the walls were an invitation one could not guard against. They too heard what was loudest, the temples burning, and if they could hear this throbbing of the temples then they too grew as deaf as the lovers and heard nothing more, not their whispered tenderness, their stated will to live which somehow in this intense embrace needed to be stated. Perhaps the neighbor heard the eyelids close, the arms widening, the bodies desiring flight. Heard the promises which had to be made clearly simply because they had to be made. In the end, neighbors could not help but possess each other's secrets and remember what lovers themselves could not remember; the words that fell like jewels out of their mouths to measure each portion of an embrace, words laced, dipped in a fragrance soft like milk, words chiseled like stone, words with wings to touch the sky. These precious words needed witnesses to gather them into a song.

They took turns to lick one-penny stamps till the stickiness was gone, then they pasted the stamp onto the top right-hand corner of the envelope but the stamp slid down with too much saliva on it, till, of its own mysterious will it dried halfway at the bottom of the envelope, just next to the address written in a close neat hand. They closed the envelope and threw it underneath embroidered pillowcases to be posted or else forgotten. A letter to a neighbor who had left an address for Salisbury. They wrote a letter to Pholisa Nyathi, at Mbare, while knowing full well that this letter would never be answered and this neighbor had already vanished into some city-flavored, idle, irrecoverable pursuit.

Nothing has more music in it than trains.

The ease of movement, sweeping over the ground through the din and smoke and loud engines, the steam hissing into the sky and the fires blazing. So they get onto a train and find themselves in the city. It is not possible to move freely through the closely guarded train and into the curtained coaches, through its entire wailing sound, the whistle blazing and tearing the air like paper. They stay in their Fourth Class coaches where there are golden-brown benches fixed to the floor of the train, and where single mothers creep under the benches clutching their three-week-old infants whom they fold fondly on raised knees and bowed chests so they can suck some tenderness from their bodies. Whenever the train comes to an abrupt stop only the iron pedestals of the benches, and human feet, catch and hold them down. There is no light.

There are money-paying jobs in laying the tracks which go on for interminable distances, but these were taken over by others who had been here before there was any building to be done, whose lands had been grazed to make way for the railways. The tracks are already down ready to carry the people, the coal, the oranges. There are clouds of cotton and sunflower seeds too. The smell of tobacco rolled into massive bales, and cattle ready for abattoirs. The smoke slides down the windows like a solid rain.

The train comes to Bulawayo to Fort Victoria to Gwelo to Que Que to Gatooma to Salisbury. The people come from even further away. Everywhere there is an attempt to get on the train for the long trip to the city. One takes a bus from Mhondoro, where there is no train, and arrives in Hartley, and has to decide whether to go to Salisbury or Bulawayo, each of them big and growing cities. Bulawayo bigger. The Rhodesia Railways headquarters is housed there. Bulawayo is close to South Africa and that, by itself, is a full story. The decision is not easy. It is best to watch the train for several days while it sweeps in both directions, first of course to find courage to get on it, watch it swing to and fro, then simply leap on it without checking which way it is now heading. Seeing it standing still with the doors and windows open is enough to excite courage, and if it is morning, to turn the head back to see the dazzling tail of smoke blacken the sky is a miracle which makes you ponder, not what kind of sorrow is ahead, but what kind of sorrow has already died.

The fascination which has propelled them to the city is not enough to secure their survival. However, regret, if there is any, lasts only a second before they are resigned to their situation. They curse and blame the trains, then cling even more to the city. The people have come from everywhere, and absorb and learn not only each other's secrets but each other's enigmatic languages. Accent rubs against accent, word upon word, dialect upon dialect, till the restless sound clears like smoke, the collision of words, tones, rhythms, and meanings more present than the trains beating past. They laugh when meaning collapses under the weight of words, when word shuffles against word, but they know something precious has been discovered when a new sound is freed, and soothes the gaps between them.

True, they laugh at each new and distant tongue but remain curious and involved. Whatever else remains out of synchrony, they manage to greet each other in English, saying hallo, easily, as though hallo is not at all an English word. It is part of being here. Jim . . . Baas . . . Jim . . . Baas . . . Jim . . . Baas. The children in the waiting rooms see this truth and it amuses them to endless mimicry. They take torn cotton sleeves which they tie into a band across the eyes, then call for Jim. Jim answers from under the benches, from behind the shoulder, from behind the garbage cans, from everywhere but where the small arms are reaching out to find him. So Baas knocks against the benches and hits against the walls and the darkness. Calling for their fathers who bear names like Sixpence, Tickey, Teaboy, and Lucky.

The city is like the train. It too is churning smoke in every direction, and when looked at closely, it too is moving. There is something strange in that even if one has not dreamed of any kind of success in coming here, getting back on the train in order to go back to an earlier safety feels like failure, like letting go. The past is sealed off no matter how purposeful it has been, even if the past is only yesterday. It cannot be consulted for comparison. There will be questions to be answered when one returns, simple questions such as what Bulawayo looks like. To answer adequately there is need to stay longer, to be part of it, to examine the pavements closely even if one stays safely away from them, to look through opaque windows and hurry right past to another destination where nothing urgent has to be attended, except waiting.

They are here to gather a story about the city. Upon returning, perhaps the story can be told by simply producing something one can clasp in the hand, something miraculous that will provide concrete evidence not only about the city but the bearer too. So it takes time to decide to go back, what with searching for the concreteness which has no clear name. Time swallows time as it becomes abundantly clear that the miraculous something cannot be easily found. The only concreteness is the pavement, and that they cannot even walk on.

So the most congested place is the railway station, with its waiting rooms, where people linger for months with nowhere to lodge. With no direction. They move from room to room and tuck their semiprecious belongings under the wooden benches, on the cement floors. The benches are wide and go round the three walls. The front wall is an open archway, with only a partial cover. A smaller arched opening without a door leads to the next waiting room and another to the next in a straight line but it is not possible to walk through each door right to the end of the rooms. There are obstacles. Bodies lie in rows, raised from the ground, but there is not enough room so the floors are soon covered with bags and restless bodies. From waiting room, to waiting.

At night it is dark inside, with no light except what falls in from the platform while the trains are still moving. A roof juts out from the waiting rooms to the next platform, so the light of the moon is lost. In the distance, in the early hours of the morning emerge handfuls of dim light. Dangling like pendulums, handheld lamps from the men inspecting the tracks, moving slowly, up and down, dancing like fireflies. A blunt light pulses through the thick glass of the lamp now covered with condensed air, the fog of the morning appearing above the corrugated roofs of the worksheds on the remote end of the station, like steam from a cauldron, way beyond the last platform. The rail tracks sparkle with cold, with a coagulating dew hanging down the metal edges, sliding past the thick paste of black oil encrusted along the metal joints and bolts. The lamps walk searchingly in the quiet night. The feet stamp the broken gravel stones and slide down the raised ground where the tracks are laid, the other men step, beat upon the wood in regular practiced footsteps, delivering a soft silent heat to their knees.

Then the ground trembles like an earthquake as the train approaches. The hand placed flat on the floor of the waiting room feels the ground pound like a heartbeat. The train finally is coming. And those who have not found a place along the benches soon learn to sleep through that frenzied beat. The nights are dark and stale with breathing and the congestion of unwashed and hungry bodies. Even here, a child is born.

There are always many explanations for arrivals. Some had followed a relative here, not knowing that the place was so big you could not find anyone without providing a fixed address and firm directions. Instead of returning to their homes they linger, just happy to be near the chaos. Even without participating, they are also part of the whole. Their suitcases grow dank with unwashed clothes, till they abandon the suitcases beside the large metal garbage cans, then eventually everything is discarded except the sound of approaching trains.

The sound links them to distant and lost places. There are possibilities here. Something can change and make them part of things that are growing. Often a guard comes and drives them from the waiting rooms, and asks them to produce tickets to show which train they are waiting for, or show the money with which they intend to buy a ticket—their skin burning, they flood out with their small utensils but return one by one. They go to the edges of the city but come back. There is nowhere else but the waiting room.

Others find jobs while the rest stay where they are and let time remove hunger. They welcome the newly arrived and press their backs further against the wall so that these too can find room. Each time, there is the joy of witnessing the wonder in the eyes, the surprised face which for the first time wanders under the streetlights.

The station dwellers see it necessary to give away every possible adventure to the newcomer so that they can lay claim on something unique to themselves. All they can claim is being here first. So to prove it, they describe the city in detail: the heels of black women clicking red shoes against the pavement and holding matching bags close to their bodies clad in tight slacks; the smoothness of transparent silk blouses swishing against black skin, bras, and ultrasheen pantyhose; black women's faces turned white and soft like milk, smooth; the large city halls where on a weekend you can stand on tiptoe and see images of embracing lovers crossing the screen, or a white man in a cowboy hat ride a horse and whip naked boys from the wheels of his wagon; to describe a teacup, that is something else, it is necessary to creep up and peep through windows or wander into the First Class waiting rooms in order to say saucer with the right meaning; they tell of the newspapers printed daily and sold from street corners, then, at the end of the day, the newspapers are discarded at every street corner; in every police Jeep patrolling the city streets are white men with batons, ready to use them.

They warn the newcomer about the rules of pardon, the whole notion of being here and not being here. Just living. Lobengula Street where they can see Asian families running the shops.

They tell of the numerous women who live in the alleys and cloistered night bars where they can lean on a long-lost shame, away from the bright light. The drinking places where liquor is sold by the bottle, secretly, to black women, by bowtied black men who run shops which they own—tight cells with a single cylinder of light masked with dirt, flashing gloomily from above. In that gloom, female legs protrude from under a three-legged metal table above which men wearing red and ragged berets play cards, and argue, and pull knives which they point at each other, threaten and wheedle, while coins jingle and roll off the rusted table tops. A woman stands against the wall and dangles an almost true love, gazing with affection at the bowed shoulders of the men while she takes slow splashing sips of illegal liquor from a flat palmsized bottle encased in a crumpled plastic bag. A woman sits on the floor with knees raised off the ground and her large arms pressed on her knees while an empty bottle lies discarded under her thighs, the skirt trailing in folds behind her is all the reason she thinks she is ready for a lasting embrace. Beside her from up high drops a brimless black hat, above her, the man leans way back low and downs a full bottle of fresh milk.

These women say whatever is on their minds and whenever it is on their minds. They hate misunderstandings so they repeat every word, laugh, and fail to apologize. Apologies are unpleasant, and as far as they know, involve bending the knees right down and coming back up; this, of course, they no longer have the strength for. The liquor is clear like water but burns all the desire from their tongues. The men love this burned-out desire and follow them home where they inhale each false promise and love these already bending knees, going down, the careless sleeve lying off the shoulder, the missing syllable at the end of every word, the endless pure loss of gravity.

The women, dizzy and spellbound, walk through the night and past the factories and refineries which make nothing but sugar. They might hate the smoke but they like this astonishing dedication to sweetness and so they move a little faster. They skip over the thick stems of burned cane which have fallen from large trucks in the afternoons. The strong sugary scent claims the morning air and sobers them a little, bringing a kind of harmony to their swinging footsteps, to their hips and arms, and it is as unnecessary as time to bring the same arm up and wipe the pain breaking free from their eyelids. Rather, they listen genuinely as a long-ing long forgot slips between their empty legs and stays there like a priceless secret while they walk on. They smell the sugar burn. Smoke curls out of six towering thermal pillars and hides the stars. The women think of nothing too serious, just burning coal and burned sugar cane.

nine

Deliwe hated policemen.

She hated the black policemen. She said they were not only capable of eating their own vomit but slicing open the stomachs of their own mothers. Otherwise, why would they accept jobs in which the only pleasure was to ride Humber bicycles down the streets, push women into police vans, and lead dogs salivating for black blood. Never mind that everyone saved each hard-earned coin to own a Humber and how dizzying it was to watch someone balance their entire body on such treacherous-looking metal. Never mind that. Never mind any of it. These policeman were evil. She hated them and that was not a secret she, or anyone else, could keep.

Her small house on Sidojiwe E2 was a hive of activity even in the small hours of the morning. She had partitioned the front into a porch and planted a thorn-bush hedge all round. In winter, the bush bloomed yellow seeds which were long and dangled with a juice thick like syrup, pouring out of their cracks. On Sunday afternoons she opened her front door wide in order to hear her pot cook on the Primus stove, and sat calmly on the porch on one of the empty beer crates which said, in large black print, Southern Rhodesia. The possession of this crate was a crime for which she could be punished.

Deliwe had once been locked up for a whole night in a police cell for selling alcohol and moreover in a dwelling. She threw her head back and laughed like a madwoman when she was told that this square shelter with its falling roof, its colorless weak walls, and nowhere to make love to a man, was a house. That was when the policeman slapped her. Afterward, Deliwe always turned her left ear to hear what you had to say. She never explained that the deafness in her right ear was caused by the beating she received during her detention. She continued to make her own liquor and sell it. The police had already told her the skokiaan she served to her customers destroyed the lungs. "Have you ever opened a black man to see if he has lungs inside?" she asked. They hit her again. A black policeman followed her home and offered to heal her wounds. She spat at him. He slapped her and told her he would keep her cell clean of cockroaches till he came back to collect her. And left her door ajar.

When she returned to Sidojiwe E2, she carried on as though no one had disturbed her. "Everyone is allowed to have visitors," Deliwe answered whenever she was asked if she did not fear the police. Deliwe was not even a large woman to look at. A fifty-year-old woman, she was slender and tall as though she did not eat anything. A red scarf was always tied over her hair, not because she was modest enough to cover her white hairs. No. She had no white hairs. She had to keep her head covered because she was busy. The knot at the back of her head kept all her plans together. She had other things to think about. Nothing in her body told you she had such courage, except her eyes, which held scorpions.

The scorpions had risen in her eyes after she fell out of the police van on her way to the police station. She did not want to go and insisted she had not committed a crime by having visitors in her house. She did not like to be caged all the way to the station and said she would walk. She was trying to jump out while it was moving at full speed. She fell out and rolled all the way to the side of the road where she lay stunned by her own impulse. The driver stopped meters away and reversed into her body. She watched the wheels turn and the scorpions kept mounting in her eyes. The wheels kept turning till they pressed against her body. They threw her back inside the van and handcuffed her to the floor. She lay on the floor for the entire trip. Deliwe had kept her eyes like that and it frightened some and made others, like Phephelaphi, mad with hope.

Deliwe's house was one of several shebeens where one could buy alcohol from sunrise to sunrise, and stay there in the house to drink it for the entire time. Four candles burned from four sides of the room, and Deliwe was always warning her customers not to burn down her curtains with the candles. This referred to a thin torn cloth which was kept down all day. It covered a small square window with a tiny front ledge where she kept her matches and unused candles. She tossed the cloth up to see if there was lightning in the streets so that she could quickly hide her liquor. Lightning referred to the speeding vans which raided the neighborhood in the early hours of the morning looking for evidence of deceit. They looked in the wrong places and at the wrong time of day: deceit is carried in the eyes, it is witnessed in daylight. Because of these night raids Deliwe always went to bed as naked as the day she was born. She liked to see the surprise in a policeman's eyes. She took her time dressing while the policeman shouted and called her a miserable wicked woman.

The day Phephelaphi went to Deliwe's house Fumbatha had been away for a week. She was free of his protection and gloried in an unexpected and absolute surprise. She felt a sense of wholeness in making a decision without him. She wanted to hear the music they called Kwela. After all, she had already met Deliwe herself, briefly, among the vegetable stalls and they both lived on Sidojiwe E2. A mere accident of a meeting in which Phephelaphi heard Deliwe's raised voice, harsh and determined, state with no doubt that this voice was obedient only to Deliwe. Then she saw the firm knot, red, at the back of Deliwe's head. Then Deliwe, laughing, but nothing could hide the scorpions in her eyes. Her voice grew fierce as she turned her neck and emitted a sound slow and deliberate, which had no words in it but rejected every insinuation of opinion on anyone else's part. The sound was an instant intake of air between the tongue, the cheek, and some other part of Deliwe's body which only she could command. In an instant, Phephelaphi felt that the sun rose and set with Deliwe. She admired every word which fell out of her mouth. She wanted to pick up the word and put it in her own mouth. So dearly was Phephelaphi charmed. Deliwe laughed at the women selling the vegetables and said they were the laziest people she had seen in Africa. Her Africa meant Sidojiwe E2. Phephelaphi hid her basket of tomatoes and followed her all the way to her house like a starved animal. She understood Deliwe's impatience with the selling of dried vegetables.

On that first day Deliwe was only interested in cleaning the floor of her room and making the house good for her visitors. She swept out bottle tops and pieces of torn newspaper from inside the house. She retrieved some of the folded newspapers and placed them between the pages of a Bible. She threw the Bible on the other side of the floor as though she did not want to see it again. Phephelaphi was puzzled. Deliwe ignored her and took a jacket which she said a man had left behind. She hung it at the back wall, but first she searched through all the pockets. "He is a poor man," she said, and moved the jacket to the darkest corner of the room. "If he is not back for it in two weeks, I will sell it at the market."

Phephelaphi promised to come back when there was music. Deliwe laughed. She wondered what Fumbatha would say about a woman he guarded like a hawk coming to her shebeen. Deliwe knew Fumbatha and had seen how he treasured Phephelaphi above every other woman he had known. He claimed he had pulled her out of the water like a fish and there was every evidence to prove that this story was true. Phephelaphi did not possess a single blemish and no other woman would find one no matter how hard she searched, and if she did, then she would certainly have had to place it there in malice. Deliwe ignored her promise that she would come again.

Though Deliwe was curious about this fine pair and their devotion, she thought it best not to encourage Fumbatha's anger toward her. After all, he had found a woman whose body was all promise, breasts firm and rounded, a voice so soothing soft no other woman could exceed its charm and no men ignore its plea. Fumbatha would definitely not be amused by Deliwe's interference. He was a man who made, and unmade, his own mind. However, the matter was resolved differently because Phephelaphi was a woman who chose her own destination and liked to watch the horizon change from pale morning to blue light. She thought Deliwe was some kind of sun, and herself some kind of horizon. Deliwe was unaware of her own attraction and failed to look up and see the bliss, the ecstasy, the freedom spreading its wide wings over Phephelaphi's body as she stood watching her. She failed to observe that her hands thrust into each of the man's pockets was all the sign Phephelaphi needed to come back, her head reeling, again. She had underestimated Phephelaphi's need and determination.

Fumbatha knew and disliked Deliwe. He said she was teaching young boys to forget their troubles. He hated her ways, he said. She was the sort of woman to make a man crawl as though he had never walked on his own two legs. She liked to see a man fall on his knees. Phephelaphi wondered what Fumbatha truly meant. She had made up her own mind to visit Deliwe without letting Fumbatha know.

On the day she has chosen to visit Deliwe's house, she dresses in her best clothing and walks carefully along Sidojiwe E2. It feels like the longest and darkest street in Makokoba. She walks frightened, with the stars diving down from the sky. She is wearing a flaring white skirt underneath which is a stiff petticoat which she has dipped in a bowl of warm water thickened with sugar and then ironed hot till it dried. A white butterfly, her waist a tight loop.

She is thrilled to be walking in the night on her own to Deliwe's house. Phephelaphi has waited until very late in the night. She arrives safely at the house and walks into a cloud of thick smoke in which the light from the candles tries to penetrate. The burning ends of cigarettes form red dots throughout the room and trace the up and down glowing movements of each arm. There is a leisured atmosphere, as though the people inside have never heard of a problem in this part of the world. Phephelaphi hears their humming voices as she approaches the room, no, she feels the soft voices like the tip of a feather moving in circles over her arms. On this strange and joyous evening she feels everything on her skin, including the caress from the brief notes of a guitar being tested at a far corner of the room.

As she enters and searches the room for Deliwe, only the outline of men's hats can be seen carving soft lines over each raised knee. Beneath the curve and line of the hat above the knee is the slender trouser, the center pressed into a sharp edge which she wants to touch with her fingers. Phephelaphi has never seen anything quite so tidy as these gathered men. She looks around anxiously for Deliwe.

They sit on low stools, the men. Now she knows why Deliwe makes a fuss about cleaning her floor to a brilliant shine. These men have pride all over their fingertips. She, Phephelaphi, is the only stranger about and suddenly she feels not complete, not ready for this encounter, her emotions too gaudy and imperfect, her experience slim as a needle. She should have been born yesterday, not today, this night, with all these men surrounding her. She is intensely aware of being a woman. A woman in a room. It is a simple fact. It is so new to her. Phephelaphi is more frightened than she has been by the darkness outside the door. A precipice, and she is standing right on the lip of its fall. The ground below goes on forever. The ground below is the solid rock of a woman. She can stand on it, so she lets herself fall as far as she can reach.

It is a treasure to enter this changed room. Even in the near dark she can see the top of each sharply pointed shoe, and wonders how all five toes can fit in such narrow space. It is thrilling, the shoe with its clean pointed end, the hats with the carefully turned up brim, and underneath the hat and the sole of the shoe the rising rough note of the guitar. A single rough note. A broken string.

Phephelaphi looks again at the glistening shoes flipped, raised off the floor, delicately rested down by the edge of the heel while the soft light from the candle gleams the polished leather—the laces, firm and neatly tied. Her eyes grow accustomed to the room and she pauses. She retrieves with one invisible hand one of the cushiony hats and holds it close while the guitar continues to pulse under her skin. Her mind wanders.

The jackets the men wear are long, reaching way beyond the waist. The jackets fall onto the floor where the candles burn four neat circles on each of them. She sees the colors soar; the luminous green suit, the turquoise blue, the violent red. The white suit has stolen every ounce of magic from the moon.

She is thoroughly unprepared. When the music tears into the room she almost falls to the floor with agony. It hits her like a hammer, a felled tree, even though the noise is far and low and way back beneath her eyes where it trickles away like a stream. Stunned, wounded, she holds on to the door while she listens to the stream grow into a river and shift every boulder, every firm rock in her body. It leaves a tunnel, an empty tunnel she fills with a far-flung desire. A yearning. She can swim, but she prefers to sink deep down and touch the bottom of the river with her naked body and her stretching arms.

She remains at the door but closes it gently, like a lid over a precious liquid. She watches as a man raises a shining instrument from his knees to his tongue. He rises lovingly and his shoulders smooth the air into the shape of his own body, and his jacket falls obediently behind him and cuts the bottom of his knees. Neatly. The cloth is like skin.

He prepares to play. His arms upward. His eyes closed. His twin elbows pushing every other thought away. And a hurricane of tender tones meets every ear, escalating, on and on. The room grows quiet like a rainbow, all voices cease as though the man standing up is a sign, a command. If there is symmetry in his trim dress, there is absolute harmony in his song—his music is healing.

He plays and lets off a mournful tune which has no beginning at all, just a presence which makes Phephelaphi feel she has heard this song before, that she has lived and breathed in it. She creeps to a corner in the room and kneels down into the sound which is low like a whimsical wind, almost inaudible at the beginning like dry leaves, but it grows gently up and she is able to cross the distance it asks her to cross and to touch, finally, before it reaches the ground, the hand falling down from the doorway, to keep it there.

She raises the slender arm high up to the top of the doorway and keeps it there, for the longest time that she can, that her heart can, before the pounding in her head grows to a pitch which she cannot bear. She lets go not because she wants to but because she has to. She sees again the hand falling right down to the floor and the well of misery in her own heart fills her with wonder.

She forgives Emelda knowing how difficult it is to be a woman, to fly with a broken limb. She misses her in a solitary echo, a beat too near the bone. She knows this song, its every touch. She wonders whether it was not Getrude she should have forgiven rather than Emelda. She wants to laugh except the room is so new to her, and no, there is a hurt somewhere which is still hers . . . between the falling hand and not knowing if the blood will follow the wound and how long it will be before the blood follows the wound, and, should she touch anything but the arm? She had not minded the death at all. Just the blood taking so long to make the dying true. And afterward, her own tears taking too long to surface in order to make true the blood. The longing not there at all. Nothing inside her except the furrow, the groove, the trough, the unbounded channel which the river had found. No tears now, not in the sound which offers such empty and harrowing spaces in her mind. Finding Emelda. Emelda.

Phephelaphi brings her right arm over her chest and holds down the hurt. Finally, she has found Emelda.

t e n

Fumbatha sees the sky peel off the earth; that is the distance between the land and the sky. This hill is a surprise.

A hand swings forward and throws a heavy load. Another picks the tune and adds a word. A pristine word to a song makes everything poignant. The birth of a word is more significant than the birth of a child.

They sing as brick pounds from hand to hand to hand. Thrust or thrown. Carried, lifted, and raised; thrust, carried, and raised.

Fumbatha is among the men who stand in a long line beside the truck. They stand one behind the other reaching forward to the place which has been chosen and marked for the new building. The place is located uphill so the many men, further on, appear like a string of beads, slight and fragile while bending forward and reaching back along their waists to receive the bricks, and their heads a rapid motion, each man continuously extends and withdraws his arms—each brick is carried with the astonishment of an entire body, borne in symmetry.

They sing when their breathing can allow, their chant and pitch hard like charcoal, their throats like burning wood. Their faces a mask for their voices. Eyebrows vanish into creased foreheads. Arms are smooth like burnished stone, sweat trickles over this glistening skin, and down the deep ridge from the base of the neck, a channel of sweat. The bending hollowed back, flesh and bone, rippling like wings.

The task is accomplished working speedily and with little pause, their bodies toss and whirl. Black wood in a flood moving in full circles. If there is a shore along this river it is not yet a shelter but something hostile. It is an unknown possession. An obstacle against which the bodies are blindly thrust, and thrust again. Wood floats on water: blazes in flame.

Above these figures of working men rises the boundary of thick coiled wire which partitions the land. There are no trees except stunted shrubs, and mounds of jutting gray rocks dug from the ground. The rocks absorb the heat like furnaces. Colorful lizards gather on the rocks, spread flat like wounded fingers, primal hand-marks on stained rocks. The men will soon move the rocks to make room for the new structures. And the lizards, unsure of the comfort of human hands, will sacrifice their peaceful dormancy for safety. The world tilts. The open hand will close.

Unseen and only felt. Beyond the piercing sky. Higher and higher. Beyond and after the dreams of white men have replaced the shrubs and the rocks and the brilliant silver sky. Some place, beyond each swing of the arm and the guilty collapse of the knees, after the shared vibration and accent of each wailing song, waits the men's own unmistakable shame, oozing like a muddy waterfall.

Told what to do, where to stand. They shape the future with their own callused hands. They mix cement in wheelbarrows and paste brick to brick. The day is measured by the height of a shadow falling from each wall. Bold structures emerge.

Fumbatha lifts brick after brick with the men, but his thoughts have moved away past the sky blue, soft, above his shoulders. He thinks deeply of Phephelaphi. He must keep her close. Somehow. All the time. He must make her belong. He understands her better now and watching her each day, he is convinced that she needs more. "I want to become a nurse at the hospital," she says, "I am sending in my application." She has all the qualifications to enter the course, and the absurdity to imagine—without ever having seen the evidence—that her application would be considered. She claims a schoolteacher from United School had once told her that by the end of 1946 black applicants would be accepted for nursing training. The issue has even been debated in parliament.

Fumbatha does not encourage her, instead, he reminds her of what they share. "We are happy together. I work. I take care of you. It is not necessary for you to find something else." He insists on her unwavering loyalty. He mistrusts the city which does not understand the sort of triumph a man and a woman can find and share in their solitude. Does no one know that he is willing to die on the palm of Phephelaphi's hand?

It is important that she understand his fear, not his constraint. United School on Church Street had been built in 1903. By 1935 the school was solidly there and being poor and curious was all one needed to enter its doors and learn. No matter what disarray attended her, Phephelaphi had a mother who made sure she attended school.

Getrude, who was always ready and running, had prepared whatever avenue there was for escape. She had no suspicion about open doors, she only took care that the tip of her shoe remained ungrazed.

United School provided opportunity and comfort. Phephelaphi had gone there from Sub A to Standard Six. This is the highest level Phephelaphi has reached in her education and as far as she is concerned it is all that is required for her to train as a nurse.

It is not the being a nurse which matters, but the movement forward—the entrance into something new and untried. Her heart rises in an agony of longing. She is going to be the first to train, if the occasion allows her. "No one will come knocking on my door telling me to apply," she says to Fumbatha. "And if we do not apply, will anyone know that we are interested?" she asks.

There finally can be some use for the little that she knows and has gathered. Her emotions a flurry of excitement and curiosity, she speaks to Fumbatha with a hopeful tone, believing that he will understand her immediately; he surprises her. Fumbatha forbids it. "We have our life together," he repeats. She turns her head away and lets her arms fall heavily. They share a silence which Phephelaphi hopes she will never have to suffer with him again, and which Fumbatha knows he can never endure without suffocating. He wants to love her without risk, but Phephelaphi had been born in the middle of Makokoba, her idea of progress includes United School. What comes after that, is now the nursing school. Fumbatha wonders if she will apply. Phephelaphi wonders if he can stop her.

The sky releases him. Fumbatha hears the men heave beside him and returns his attention to the work. They discard memory like rotten fruit while they touch the sliding loose soil, clutch roots and firm elements, learn to lean on silent rocks dug from under the earth. They are consumed but not resigned. Surrender, physical, visible, sharing the same axis of rotation as resistance. Each with an equal momentum, each with the possibility ending: suddenly, abruptly. Each an emotion.

An axis is an anchor, an origin, not the emotion itself. Emotion is much more charged and cannot be fastened to a single location; it consumes the whole body. The body relents like a canoe keeling over in turbulent streams, then skims the surface of the water to a welcoming border, without sinking; something about the weight of wood, the apex, the slender vessel, and the position of the drowned.

In water, an oar held firm in one place builds a current that makes a whole vessel turn in another direction: the power of inertia.

Fumbatha's body bends to pick up an instrument and his shoulders swing to throw an object; this is not submission. An anger is gathered in the most minute solitude of his mind, in the folds of history most charitable to oneself. It is simultaneous with the forced action, it precedes and follows in the familiar way in which sound follows the fall of an object on a hard surface. A relationship is built between the sound and the object. But once we have heard the same fall, the same object meet the same surface, then it is no longer necessary to witness the object fall in order to associate the sound with the object. The emotion behind the motion can be anticipated like sound; it can be retrieved in a moment when eyelids are closed to the light and the shape of a single incident recorded. This is the perfection of memory.

Two arms swing and thrust forward. The head bends. The muscles quiver, taut with hostility. Something is freed but collides with something else less hurried and more pardonable, a dream perhaps. Another word enters the air and absolves what is hidden beneath each moving arm, what builds up under the brow. This word draws another and the two make honey. We are here. This is said urgently and with wisdom. We are here. The here of it and the now of it make the honey.

Rocking and touching, each man holds on to the word the other has offered and each word raises the moment. The birth of a word, violent, mute. They are pitched against an opposite world so they plunge and pull. Each utterance is purposeful, each silence true like absent desire. Impotent with unspoken words, they weave forward, and bend. They lean backward, and bend. Something burns on their lips, yes, like honey.

Their voices spread evenly like the buzzing of bees. The shovels beat the ground and they delve the earth and make a grid. They shovel and hollow the earth and sing. They are undeterred and keep their eyes on the shovels and the bricks and the cement in order to create what does not belong to them. Time has unmade them. Placed them uniquely here. This place, this time. A buzzing like bees, but beneath the pollen, between their own feet, they make music.

They heal the day and move in keeping with each task. Their shoulders bowed to the ground from where they build the wall till it is higher than any of them. They sing higher than anything they have built and between all this is the grass burning and forming a cloud on the horizon. The ground is cleared and the land itself burns. A thick black ash rises and falls toward the men whose hands are filled with the work. Their faces are covered with the grass now lighter than pollen, and to the touch, it feels cleaner than drops of water. This is the substance of words which rise and fall, like soot finely laid on a blade of grass, on the tip of a feather, on the crest of anger.

In the beginning, in the early morning, their voices trickle and hold together like a stream; in the afternoon like something equally sweet, laden, with the sound of bees in it.

Their voices hold together, gathering slowly as the day wears on. It is not in the voices, their refusal, not in the voices at all because the voices have the quality of grains pouring out of a basket, a winnowing fall, the chaff sweeping into the wind, the heavy seeds contained to bursting. The sound of seeds falling in a wind.

Yellow dust patterns the horizon; wings of a bird land on a branch; a feather falls from the height of a tree. These are voices.

It is evening. Fumbatha rests his body against the dry ground.

eleven

Finding herself, that was it. Phephelaphi wanted to be somebody. Not once but twice, thrice, she visited Deliwe at her house
and stood at her doorway and lingered again in the cigarette
smoke, and placed her arm over her stomach where she nursed a
wailing hurt, gathering there like a spring, because there was a
longing there, burning. Fumbatha could never be the beginning
or end of all her yearning, her longing for which she could not
find a suitable name. Not a male hurt or anything like it. She
missed Fumbatha whenever he was away but this hunger she felt
was new. Not on her skin or anywhere she could touch. It was a
feeling rising like tears. She wanted to do something but had no
idea what it could be, what shape it offered for her future.

She could not stop the longing even though she heard the

water lapping against the edges, against the rim, as though she was some kind of river and there were things like flooding which could take place inside her body. It was full desire because she liked the lapping on the rim and the liquid falling down her arms, falling, down to her knees.

It was an urge. Not knowing what could cure it, she let it spread into all of her like an ache. Not Getrude anymore whom she missed, though she had always wanted her and now Getrude was gone with a finality which Phephelaphi could no longer grieve. Finding herself, that was it. She missed Getrude, the simple manner in which she lifted her arm loosely like a rope and brought her elbow round to her ear and listened to it. When Phephelaphi was younger it never failed to make her laugh. Getrude listened to the bend on her arm as though there was a message there and then she also asked her to listen, but try as she might she could not move her own arm all the way round, so she brought Getrude's elbow to her own ear and listened. A childhood game. She heard the hollow fluttering of wings, heard the wind blow softly through those slender bones. Phephelaphi had never been able to twist her own arm all the way round like that, it was the sort of lightness that belonged solely to Getrude. If she could, she would. So they both laughed and let their bodies be.

Getrude, who had a dress for going to town and a dress for staying home, and who made this distinction important enough that the dress for going to town was always on a metal hanger and placed on a peg near the open window so that it got some full-time air. That dress. A hugging sort of dress which pronounced the ooze and flow of all her energy. She needed nothing else but that dress for neighbors' heads to turn and curse and feel their privacy had been violated and their own attraction put to test, she made trust turn to cinders and birds to fly from hedges, and then a sparkling reckless warmth flowed from Getrude's long endless arms, the curve of her shoulder seemed mightier than paradise.

A pale-green dress faded under the armpit but which looked all the more delightful for its aging parts, it had circles spreading from under her arms and she let it be. The seam loosening. The thread ready to tear. A large hem, limp, dangling past her knees like ripe things, the stitching on it so carelessly sewn it showed even though it was the same enviable green as the fabric. It was the buttons though, more than all else, which silenced anybody's look and stare; the glowing buttons whose full intense color was sharper than that of the fabric and caught all there was of the sun in order to split her body into two bright halves; Getrude looked captivating from whichever symmetric side her figure was considered. She was a heart beating.

Perhaps Phephelaphi should have kept the dress or at least tried it on before destroying it; it was that single wound which she was not interested in wearing. She had enough to consider without wearing another woman's wound. Phephelaphi remembered how Getrude had arrived home late and slumped on the bed still wearing the same clothing. Getrude never fell on the bed like that without changing into something more usable, not her best pale-green dress crumpling like that. Instead she announced that she was tired, lay down, and slept on top of the bed. She got up, in the middle of night, as well dressed as she could ever be. Walking in her sleep. Ready to be surprised. The buttons on the front of her dress went from below her neck all the way to the bottom of her knees, large green buttons that tucked neatly into their crocheted hooks.

Even as a shadow in the night Getrude made Phephelaphi forget everything else but Getrude. It was not the dress, it was how Getrude moved inside the dress, floating forward as though she owned all of Jukwa Road though it was obvious that all she owned she carried with her. She had her qualities. She could cast a look at another woman which stunned by its directness, its superior and gifted disdain, its absolute ambush of anything anyone had to say. It was not much but it was something. No one could survive Getrude's curl of the eyebrow, the dainty crease on her forehead which looked plain deliberate, her tightened lip, her slow and purposeful stride. And of course, the full miracle of her body. Unlike other women, she needed neither nylons nor a good heeled shoe to give her grace. Neither powder nor Pond's. No earrings or other ornament of appeal. Just her lazy footsteps and her exquisite body which had suckled only one child and not felt any of the scars.

She should have held on briefly to the dress. Only a day. Only a few days before 1946, so what was wrong with waiting another week and burning the dress at midnight. Time enough. It was the policeman who confused her with his disinterested tone and the way he stood there as though he had all day and she could easily be the most important person on earth and he had his cap in his hands as though she was truly important. That confused her because she knew the matter to be different. He did not even know her mother's name, and when he did not, he neither cared nor asked but scribbled whatever suited the corpse. Phephelaphi knew nothing about policemen except that it was a safe and proven habit to hate them. When they asked a question, it was best to help as little as possible. If they offered help, to run. She did not know how to deal with this hat-in-the-hand policeman who stood outside the door where she could still see her mother falling, on that same door, carrying the same dress she wore, handing it to her, waiting, watching her read the letters on it and search inside the bag which said Emelda.

Fumbatha. She missed him but her emotion was too lonely. Now she remained alone after he entered the room. She longed to tell him of her feeling but she feared watching something die because she had caused it to. Yet, who could she be and how, where could she be and with what wings. She had a craving for something sweeter than peach or any of her favorite fruit, a longing which made her trace the frame of Deliwe's doorway with her fingertips and search the room for that low-down buried hurt she understood to be there, inside her, inside that jive and music she had discovered. The abiding hurt. She felt again the men gaze at her after the music stopped, their laughter and teasing, and one of them pulled her to him and threw her onto his lap, twisting her over like a feather and she slipped. He caught her silently and let her be.

The rest of the men had laughed a graceful laughter which she did not mind at all, which sought a fine balance between things. Or so she thought. They talked long into the night about music, about gold mines across the Limpopo River where some of them had been, and this memory glittered in their minds and they spoke with accents which they had dragged from across the river, without drowning. And mountains with air so cold it turned to stone, and you could see this congealed air from the bottom of the mountain, a white cloud stretching past the sky. This was beautiful and made them sing a divine tune, knowing they could never have seen anything equally sublime except falling stars if they had not gone past the Limpopo to that distant land.

She did not believe any of it even after they described the mines, caverns in which they were immersed for days, for weeks. There they dig and listen to trains and sing along with that motion so that their arms are strong as steel, quick as light, pounding back and forth and pulling away.

The men praised her, described her as a lily blooming in a pool of water lush with sun. She did not mind the description, only curious because she had never seen such a thing as a flower blooming in water since all she knew was the Umguza River, certainly not the Limpopo with the rapids they described with such affection. And she, a flower blooming in water, that was she. She was bemused and listened to them describe each of her petals, a pure shining yellow that turned to an intense clean gold at the pith. Whose petals opened at morning with the sun, and folded in nighttime. She laughed to show that she did not take any of this description seriously. Instead they said her laughter reminded them of the wings of a dove and she had no idea how, and she was shy, like a sunflower bending its head. She raised her eyes to them and saw the sunflowers. It was magic to be in that room with these men who had seen something that was not flat land and thorn bushes. They spoke only because they felt it an obligation of their malehood to say something that would make her feel the obligation of her own womanhood. She felt more than that. She wanted more than obligation, not a fleeting excitement among male strangers with enticing tongues and a flirtatious oneness. She wanted a birth of her own.

The man in the green suit said a woman is for loving. If you love a woman enough she will unburden herself. That is the sweetest woman there is, a woman who has been loved well enough. This was the truest woman there was and a man could live a happy life. He looked at her directly and spoke to her alone. She looked away. She wanted to raise her voice loud and say that it was not like that at all, it was that a woman must love herself enough. A woman like that is the sweetest woman there is. She believed this but could not say it. What kept her quiet was that she remained puzzled by one aspect of her belief, the question she could not answer was how a woman got to do that, how she got to love her own knees, and kiss her own elbows, how she got to feel she was all the breeze there is and all the mornings there are and all the loving there could be. And then seek something more which perhaps only another can provide, and love a man simply because she could, and indeed something in him made her heart beat, and yes, her knees weak with the flow of his tender caress. Finding herself, that was it. She did not know what this entailed.

After that she could look at a man without falling or seeking shelter in his eyes, then she could be with him without burning like a dry petal, the way she was burning because a man loved her and she felt caught in a storm and could simply drown, though, indeed, she loved him back. She wanted other conditions for missing his presence. It was about loving her own eyebrows before he had passed his fingers over them and showed her that she had a smile that was tucked down on the edges, before he said she creased her eyebrows when she laughed, before he offered her the smoothness on her arms like a gift and gave her the straight lean hips she already owned, and made them hers. She wanted the time before time, before her legs felt empty and useless without him in them, before all that. She wanted the sense of belonging before that kind of belonging which rested on another's wondrous claim, being herself because she was a flower blooming in her own green pool, to be able to pick the flower which was herself from the water before he reached out his own strong arm and did all that for her and made her feel empty and waited upon. She did not want a man crossing the Limpopo and returning home with her green pool and her flower and plucking away at her petals and breaking her green stem. And if she was a flower and all the water dried and he did not water her garden, what then, since she knew nothing about any of it, not even what kind of flower she was, but only some kind of water plant a stranger told her about after his own long journey through some twin hills somewhere in the distance she had not yet traveled. This was dry land, she knew that. She had to find what she could here, from within her own land, from her body. She opened her hand and searched. A petal. Buried in water. She held her breath and swam to shore. This she could do and did.

Phephelaphi did not know how to express all her wishes to the man in the green suit so she did not answer, and instead paused. She listened and kept quiet and saw the gold, and the swaying twin hills with a valley in between, grooved, wet with newborn things. She wondered how she could find the root of a tree instead of its branches, and like these men, cross the Limpopo to recover a glittering memory. How did a woman claim a piece of time and make it glitter. How does a flower bloom when it is buried in water. How did she listen to the sound of trains when she was not burrowing the earth for true gold?

The room Fumbatha and Phephelaphi share is situated
among some of those houses on Sidojiwe E2 made of asbestos
sheets, all five walls, which includes the roof. These are shelters.
Living is a matter of keeping everything intact, the mind together
too because there is so much living to be done. One room. Four
corners. These walls are borders. A retreat where one may be
naked without shame, and touch another willingly without the
obvious presence of prying and sympathetic eyes. Inside the walls
are metal hooks where a trouser dangles inside out, the pockets
flat and flared. A torn vest too. A heap of blankets on one end.
Another naked body on the ground. Some cooking utensils are
on a raised wooden pedestal which is lined with old copies of the
Bulawayo Chronicle. The damp smell of worn-out wet shoes fills

the room. A chamber pot. Melting candles and burned-out matchsticks in a wooden tray. Eggshells.

Fumbatha has been inventive in making secure their shelter. He has wedged a crumpled old cloth within the cracks where the walls meet and leave gaps of daylight. The cloth blocks some of the rays, so they have to climb up the sealed partition before they can fall down into the room. By late afternoon the darkness is thick like surrender. The roof is held down by ropes of thick bending wires tied down to the walls, and by heavy red bricks laid down like anchors above the roof. The walls creak in the wind and lean further sideways as though empty of belief. They remain standing, propped up by nothing more than the volatile will of the inhabitants. The walls dare not descend to the ground.

Together Fumbatha and Phephelaphi have placed pictures on the walls, mostly torn from old magazines. So inside their room they have carefully selected some pictures to make their living valid, pasted on the wall in this darkness with no possibility of vision. A newly formed football team stands beside a goalpost sponsored by the Matabeleland Entertainment Society. A black-and-white ball held carefully under the foot. A group of girls in short skirts and Afro wigs and identical red-rimmed sunglasses stare at the camera, each with the same wry smile and same knowing gaze and absolutely no doubt in their eyes, just tight tops and sparkling silver necklaces dangling a message of stunned wonder into the hidden crevices of their blouses. The painting of a ship with a figure leaping into the ocean with bound hands. Underneath, a caption says A SOWER. Living here said something about harvest, about the journey one traveled before time yielded its promise, about sowing seeds in water.

A few of the houses now have solid stoves made of iron, and the owners can cook their meals inside. The stoves have ovens where, after they have made a fire on its other side, the smell of baking bread wafts into the room. Usually, from one sheltering room to the next nestles a fire. It blazes smoke which accumulates over each wall, a thick and sooty soft paste which you can wipe off the asbestos with a finger.

Fumbatha and Phephelaphi find sudden joy on an evening when they walk down Sidojiwe E2, their hands joined together, and respond to the singing on the other side of the road where the people are gathered because as each of them went past, they heard a song clear the night of all its troubles and set the heart free, then they felt welcomed and offered their own voices too. Fumbatha and Phephelaphi are among them, glad to be part of something unplanned, something free like night.

They too gather in these small rooms which have no light at all, and sing past midnight about how deep the river is, how slow the movement of the hand that holds you back before you fall, how peaceful the places they have come from, and parting is fine if that is all that is left of loving because there is all this living to be done, some other loving more true to store, some stovetop love not to be ignored at all but nurtured, a brief pardon over some future harm not yet known so why not grieve now and get it over with, strangers to whisper mercies to in the gray streetlight, a crushed black hat tipped against the noonday sun, train whistles rising high into the sky, the long handle of a pot held down with a long loose sleeve, the cooking fires where the women hover and laughter tumbles in unlit passages, bicycle wheels roll past the neglected ditches in which broken needles fall from rusted sewing machines, and abandoned razors lie above cracked full-length mirrors.

Broken scissors with plastic handles, nothing to do with these except insert two fingers into the handles and press the thumb down to test the hinge, its creak and rusty sound, below that sliding of metal upon metal is a hint of something larger; a train stops and steam rises like a calm cloud. Abandoned scissors with two broken ends and where are these tips, and when did they break and how. Somehow, this is too much to remember.

As the music soars, for Fumbatha, memory has dropped way down below the waistline like a tide, collapsed, and only the steam whistles rise up into the sky freer than birds. He holds tight to Phephelaphi, knitting both their hands, as the people sing and their voices mingle with distant as well as instant needs now recalled, now forgotten. They sing of beautiful mountains encased in a bright vibrant mist, hills with sharp peaks whose tops only doves have witnessed and memory touched, hills with cobwebs pulling for miles and miles and glinting with rainbows from morning suns, noonday suns, moon-night suns and finally, the whispered voices of butterflies. He holds her securely.

Butterfly valleys tapering gently into a wilderness of bloom where everything lingers, grows, and is watered with dew, where a swarm of leaves tosses tender veins against the wind and a chorus of birds sinks into the horizon of a disappearing sun. Magnificent blue wings like an azure morning, flapping away and away. Time is inaudible.

Fumbatha and Phephelaphi long for an innocence they can touch; feet move smoothly over the ground as they follow the movements of a guitar at the back of the room and a wailing rending flute which sways way beyond memory and proud love. They dance with a joy that is free, that has no other urgency but the sheer truth of living, the not-being-here of this here-place. They know their desire to be true. Fumbatha and Phephelaphi dance together in perfect harmony, they swing sideways and up and let all their hurt expand, then watch in whispers as the men clap palm against palm against naked thigh.

The room explodes. Fumbatha and Phephelaphi stand back against the walls.

Two agile female dancers pull their white cotton skirts with blue dots high up and hold them way over their swinging waists then collide with the music, rounded hips twisting, the body rocks with one full spasm and the neck a pillar smoothed with the bright light, their eyes close in a free caress, an evocation, their slim bodies rock back and forth, and waiting lips tremble with the desire for unborn moments, and the music is a dream too true to enter so they enter it, enter with hope, with twirling raised skirts and sizzling armpits, their heels turned outward, spinning, pushing back and front in quick dizzying steps and they leap up and land with the thudding full weight of their bodies, the sound of it louder than the music which bends their knees forward and their chests down in a crawl, the neck held high, the body up then slowly down, the calves bend, the ground is too near, the harmony too beautiful, the ground too inviting so the song pulls the body up again and swings it sideways because the song swells a fine pitch where all is deep water, plain and clear, the shoulder leaning forward toward the partner in the dance, one woman and another, the left shoulder touching, yet another, and the chain grows round the room. Shoulder to shoulder.

One room. The number of people large to bursting. To Phephelaphi the roof higher and higher. The ground bottomless. She endures the long pause in which temples beat and each step is reconsidered and adjusted to meet a falling star. Suddenly, a tune breaks and the skirt falls down, tosses a multitude of blue dots outward. The arms free to clap or click or just be. Arms hang down low pulsing to the ground and only the fingers make a sound. The song ends in laughter and joyful rest, dancers slide to some corner of the room.

The women beckon and sing lilting body songs which splice the air with a coarse and comforting spasm and place their hands on their foreheads where the sun has been beating all afternoon like a drum. Longing for the decency of night and the forgiveness of stars, their lips repeat tunes from the guitar, its string snapping, its rhythm true.

Fumbatha and Phephelaphi move outside the room and from there they listen on as song tears off song from a worn-out handmade guitar. One broken string.

Already, they miss yesterday like a newly discovered ache.

thirteen

Zandile swooped into Phephelaphi's room like an eagle. She was carrying the orange slingbag she always carried and waving a hair-ironing comb, the type with a wooden handle, the sort that you place on the flame of your paraffin stove till the metal portion is warm, then smooth the hair with Vaseline and pull it out with the comb till you can smell the hair burning. The hair is smooth like cat skin. Zandile has just borrowed the comb from a friend, and while walking back to her own house on a clear Saturday morning a kind of tenderness crept up her throat, choking her like fine dust.

She came to a standstill right in the center of a sudden whirlwind dancing in her eyes. Her vision blurred only briefly before it cleared and she could see right and her mind was decided there in the middle of Elangeni Street, the shortest street in Makokoba, which had only one house on it. This house jutted out like a bend between the end of Q Street and the bottom of Sidojiwe E2 and did not belong to either. It had been built because there was a gap of empty land there which could not be wasted. Right in front of that solitary low-roofed house with its lemon sky and two voices arguing, rising higher than smoke, something in her just said Getrude, and it was enough to make her stop immediately, and turn her footsteps and walk all the way back to Q Square, through its entire length, past Q19 where she knew a woman who had died in her sleep because a man had rejected her.

A man she cared for had not smiled back when she did, not touched her wrist on the pulsing wanting spot she asked him to, not come back home one night, and the many nights that followed. It was too simple, much too obvious a failure for her to understand and certainly more than her dove's heart could endure. It was known by her own best friend that she had swallowed a sewing needle before going to bed, all two inches of it, and followed it with water. She had left the thread on the needle hanging out of her mouth. Those who viewed the corpse said it would have been a better sight to tuck this piece of unfortunate thread under the woman's dead lips before the body was buried.

Zandile walked past that memory and past the half-built structure which was going to be called Success Stores after it was completed but had been abandoned after only the foundation had been laid down. The store would have been an opportunity for some of the first black businessmen in Makokoba. The structure had been stopped in the middle of 1942 when these same able black men were asked to enlist and fight in a war which they knew nothing about, fighting Germans and Italians. Some of them had gone to Burma. It was not a time to let black businessmen acquire distractions.

The men returned. Some. As soldiers, not heroes, blind with mistrust and dizzied by an evident defeat which belonged only to their particular experience. From 1945 they could be seen walking down any road in Makokoba, glazed and perplexed by the events of the war. Not at all proper citizens of Southern Rhodesia. With no power to choose who would govern they witness the first Railway Strike, wondering how swiftly to trust their own stirring of pride; better wages, and perhaps, the possibility of reversal. Whether they could walk on pavements or not was still being debated. It was more important for cream-colored pleated parasols to parade, for bodices clad in expensive gathered satin trains to hold sway. For bonnets and bows. Walking sticks. Top hats and coattails. Arm in arm. And fiddlers when they could.

They still could not walk on pavements. Not only did they wonder, they made suitable plans of their own which they pursued with ambition. Through this, through another harm and insight, they strove to be heard. After all, they were a majority. If each man was listened to, each man could be heard. The question they needed answered was much more urgent and vexed, not about numbers, that was simple, but about being human.

On that abandoned platform, a large board on two pillars still said Success Stores. It had been there for over a full year so no one noticed it anymore. Zandile turned left into Thandanani Street and walked quickly past No. 62 Thandanani where she knew a woman whose husband sold her to another man for the value of a bicycle wheel but she had refused to leave and instead, stood on that asbestos roof with no clothes at all to cover her own body and announced loud and clear that she preferred two bicycle wheels to one, and if anyone had two bicycle wheels to give to her husband then she would leave not only the rooftop but the house and foolishness of her husband. This No. 62 Thandanani woman could be seen outside her house any time of day, knitting whatever she could, a full candle burning beside her whether it was morning or night. Zandile walked past the candle-lit house, and turned left into L Road. Her pace slowed. She stopped humming that wonderful tune which said there are now enough girls in Makokoba, with names like Dinah . . . Melody . . . Martha . . . Eukaria . . . Memory . . . Bella . . . Jane and Julie . . .

What happened to Gugulethu . . . to Ntombenhle . . . to Zanele . . . to Ntombiyethemba . . . Nkosinomusa . . . Thandolwenkosi . . . Nkazana and Bathabile . . . those humble girls who first arrived in Makokoba back before 1930 before bus tickets did and Sunlight soap, who knew they had come here with a true and unconfused purpose, to cure the persistent loss in their men, the women who brought still clinging to their hair and eyebrows the smell of country fires and burning wood, who knew something about the bitter sweet taste of curdled sour milk, who relished the lush taste of watermelons, red inside and spotted with slippery black seeds which you suck the juice out of and toss as far as you can with the tongue, and folded under their arms some dried sweet reed whose smell and flavor stays in the mouth for as long as you do not drink water, so the men did not, instead they ate the sweet reed and stayed for days with thirsty voices, loving the combination of sweet reed and the mounting deep harrowing thirst, holding on for as long as they could and wondering when, if ever, they would taste dried sweet reed gathered from last season.

Such girls, with names like Simangele . . . Sizalelaphi . . . Ntom-bemhlophe . . . Siphetheni . . . could really cure a man's eye, mellow his thighs to a temporary retreat. Zandile stopped humming about the number of girls called Mary . . . called Liberty . . . called Gail . . . and felt again the loss she had been feeling since Getrude died and this loss made her stand in Phephelaphi's doorway waving the comb like a threat, not even looking at Phephelaphi but asking her, anyway, if she needed a place to stay till she could manage on her own. Well, she had to ask at least, if nothing else, she and Getrude went a long way. Phephelaphi could never know how but when she agreed, Zandile was relieved and received her like an unexpected gift.

There were enough girls in Makokoba but one still wondered what had happened to girls like Thandiwe ... Lungile ... Ndandatho ... Nomasiko ... Sithandazile ... Thokozile ... and Ntando. These were girls bright-eyed but soft like sunrise and much calmer than a breeze. With low and restful tones. Quiet voices which made a man feel good for something, and when she was shy before him, he felt strong for something. When she raised her milk-white eyes and smiled at him, the earth opened and he kept falling, falling down into her arms. Such girls had all but vanished. Instead, they had discovered a swinging slingbag love, a sun hat, sunglass, sunshine kind of love which burned out quicker than hope. These women had forgotten what made a man worship her footprints on the ground. And of course when she called him close and whispered something senseless which he could not fathom but dared not ask, he knelt beside her and knew no harm in her pull and embrace, in her constant murmur. She whispered, claimed him entirely. There were such moments.

All the way back to her house Zandile hummed another song which said there were enough men in Makokoba with names like Gilbert ... Stanley ... and Joe. What happened to Vulindlela and Zibusiso. Those boys with pieces of dry grass caught in their hair who knew how to keep a woman steady till all the anger, all the loving, fled from her swinging, swaying, wonderful hips. The ones who knew that you could take each of a woman's bones, one by one, from collarbone to collarbone, and blow a fine and easy tune.

Zandile now worked in a shop on Lobengula Street where she sold skin-lightening creams. By January 1946 she would have been working there for a full five years. She had decided to keep the job the same day

on which she met Boyidi and abandoned every other desire, then made
him truly hers. She had a table outside Jassats where she sat with all her
items laid neatly in rows, some in glass containers, some in tubes.
Zandile was a marvel in Makokoba, a pioneer advocate of a certain form
of beauty; she was regarded with suspicion and admiration. She would
bring some of the plastic bottles and tubes to Makokoba and sell them
to the women in the different streets. The skin on her own face was a
soft yellow like egg yolk, smooth with a transparent glow, but she could
not afford to purchase enough of the creams to rub along her arms. No
one noticed that sort of omission; there were other consuming distractions. Zandile offered the feel and texture of desire.

There was an acceptable division between the face and the body. A
mask does not need to be worn on an entire self, not under the skin but
above it, it rests between the eyes and lips, the height of the bone, the
stillness of the brow, the shape of eyes, the length of the neck, the slant
of the forehead, the patterning of hair, the channel where joy and sorrow dance. This was it. Though she went to much trouble to straighten
her hair, sometimes she still wore a wig with longer and smoother hair
on it that fell to her shoulders. That was only when she went to town, to
Lobengula Street where she worked. And lips a stunning purple to
match every possible sky.

Her slingbag had things in it like a small comb which she used in
moments when she would remove her wig and comb it out, place it
back on her head, and tuck it down into her hair with the pins. She
would do this even while sitting at her table along Lobengula Street,
with the people passing. No one noticed. There was an acceptance of
what was placed on the body and what belonged to it; the illusion was
flexible. The act of reversal spontaneous. She had a small case with
brown powder, a tiny handheld mirror, bus tickets, some loose change,
and her address written in a small handwriting. One felt such a stranger

in town, it was best to write your address down and tuck it in a safe but obvious place.

She took Phephelaphi home without having consulted Boyidi with whom she shared the house. If she had asked him he would have refused because they only had that one room, like everyone else in Makokoba. She prepared a place for Phephelaphi by taking the large wardrobe standing on one side and placing it in the middle of the room. Throughout her stay, Phephelaphi had the back of the wardrobe facing her. Zandile moved all the items from Phephelaphi's side of the room, her high-heeled shoes, her red umbrella, her lotions. Only after that did she identify and move Boyidi's things, his blue cap with the broken brim, his dirty underwear which she intended to wash next Saturday when the New Year was really over; after all, they were only a few days into 1946, so what could she do but let last year linger on. There was nothing on the horizon that she could judge as necessary or urgent to make her quicken her step. Nothing in the last year she could banish.

Zandile took her time. Boyidi's knobkerrie she placed safely under the bed. And Boyidi's identity pass she also found and opened, shaking loose its entire four folds so that his thumbprints fell all the way to the floor—each tip of the finger tangible and true, thin wavering black ink lines. She folded his fingers slowly away, with his name at the top saying Boyidi Ngwenya, and underneath where the category asked for distinguishing marks it said burn on right arm. Zandile asked aloud how, and what, could be gathered and explained about a man's touch, the tiniest wandering grooves over his fingertips. She took the pass to what had become her side of the room and placed it on the small chair along the bedside. First she had to shift the candle which was placed in a saucer in the center of that chair and close the wardrobe's double doors which had swung open as she shifted it. There were clothes kept in it, to be sure, but also unopened packets of tea leaves, maize meal, soap powder.

Zandile placed the largest item on the top of the wardrobe, a large metal dish she had bought at Jassats and which she used for bathing.

Life changed at No. 8 L Road. It did not bother Boyidi at all, to be heard, understood, shared by two women. In the night when he came home and opened the door he met the wardrobe, and curled underneath it was Phephelaphi. She pulled the blanket up beyond her neck and he watched her with a moonlit fascination falling over her closed eyelids and he did not even ask who she was. He walked past her and round to the other side of the wardrobe and lay down beside Zandile.

"I have brought Getrude's daughter. You remember my friend Getrude?" Boyidi groaned and moved closer to her. Other things worried Zandile. Boyidi had a wife when they met. But that was the past. She was almost sure that he had not had another woman since then. She kept a careful eye over him.

"Getrude died, Boyidi. I told you that last year. I have to take the girl." Boyidi shifted his entire weight to her side of the bed. He pulled his trousers off from under the blankets and threw them over the back of the chair. He could smell freshly spread Mermaid Lotion from Zandile's soft shoulders and down her neckline.

"I think we will manage. She will start helping us very soon. They need some more girls at Jassats. I will ask tomorrow if they can take her."

Before she could finish Boyidi was already parting her knees and she could feel his lips moving all the way over her neck. He said nothing to her. He saw Phephelaphi's face in a pool of moonlight and if he had answered, this is what he would have referred to. Zandile held her knees down, tight, for a while, wondering if the girl could hear the two of them, and trying, between his touch and her own heart beating, to decide how bad if at all her hearing them would be. She needed time and knew she had none. Not with Boyidi in the room, with him already pressed over her chest. She regretted making this one decision in the middle of the street the way she had done. Now what was she supposed to do? She was not going to be a mother because Getrude died and left the child to perch or fly. She wanted to explain to Boyidi all her hesitation and the possible mistake she had let creep into their lives. Perhaps she could find another place for Phephelaphi the next day. Someone else would take her. Another plan could be made as soon as she got her the job at Jassats. Phephelaphi could be on her own. All she needed was a day. Just tomorrow. There were things she needed to tell Boyidi.

"I did this for Getru—"

Boyidi placed his hand gently over her mouth and with his other arm he pulled her up and led her where he wanted to go. With a beating anxious heart Zandile followed him, his every breath, his aching sweet limbs, his motion and mood. For a long while she forgot about Phephelaphi, who was lying awake with the door open wide and the moonlight swinging in, from the sky into her waiting eyes.

As she listened, Phephelaphi wondered where hope began. With a sigh that was longer, louder, more satisfied than anything the two lovers could ever have anticipated, she rolled over and turned her back to the moon.

fourteen

Flowers blossomed in the sky. The year was 1948.

A young black woman was seen walking slowly down Sido-jiwe E2. She wore a starched and pure white dress and a white cap on her head. The cotton fabric of the dress had been repeatedly ironed. Not a single crinkle in it. Flat brown shoes. A brown handbag. Her head held up. She walked steadily. She looked important. Pins held the cap down into her smoothed hair. Poised. Clean. Purposeful. Her skin luminescent from creams. Her lips moistened with a gentle fingertip of Vaseline. She drifted into the General Mission Hospital past its stony pillars and climbed the stairs on pattering soft footfalls, as though balancing only on the tip of her shoes. Her hands tucked securely into the large front pockets of her gown. The bag swung after her past the dome

into the extended foyer, into the light of the hospital's spacious court-
yard. She stood among the green pot plants and looked up to the second
floor of the building. A doctor standing with a stethoscope over his neck
beckoned to her. She ascended the flight of stairs with her shoulders
high. The hospital had accepted its first black nurse. There would be
more.

It was two weeks after she had been accepted to train as a nurse that
Phephelaphi realized she was pregnant. She was a June Intake, the ad-
mission papers said. She had a full five months to believe and trust her
good fortune, to tell Fumbatha about it, to show him the forms that said
Miss Phephelaphi Dube, Student Nurse, and the number of her registra-
tion which came after her name, the items she should bring to the
Nurses' Hostel, which included a face towel and a toothbrush. All this.
She had a man but she was not married, so she wrote SINGLE in capital
letters where it said she ought to, where the choices were married, single, or divorced. In any case married girls were not admitted as they
could get pregnant while being trained. This would be a waste of limited
allocated funds, the Ministry of Native Affairs had decided. The conditions of training were clear. She would not be accepted if she was pregnant.

She stood in front of her shoulder-high mirror and sought her reflection. She closed the curtain covering the small window and then let
her dress drop way down to her knees and gather there. She dropped
her pink underwear too and set free a handful of baby-soft hair, pitch
black and willing. Then she was looking at each curve, at her breasts, the
nipples stiff with sudden exposure, or fear, or the child growing in her,
or all. Her navel was roused from its secret place inside her. She touched
this flawless scar, wet her finger in her mouth and brought it silently to
her navel. A cold sensation fell inward into the center of her where
everything in her had its beginning and end. She moved her finger in

circles on this patch then brought her hand over her stomach where the base swelled out, hard like a large shell. She thought about the season when she met Fumbatha and what she had said to him about holding your breath, not breathing so that you knew about survival for a true while, so she held her breath tight and did not breathe for the longest time that she could, then she let go, and it took her a long time to breathe true again. She turned her back to the mirror and looked over her shoulder and it pained her to see how her back had folded in a sweeping curve as though pulled down by her growing weight. She bent down and with a heaviness which her arms could not bear she lifted her garment and held it over her body like a shield.

She pulled out the long envelope containing all her special papers from where she had hidden it between the mattress and the springboard of the sagging bed. It was the only letter she had ever received. She read her papers over and over again till her eyes grew blind with tears. She could still hear the bicycle bell from the postman who had almost given up and taken the letter with him and had only waited because her window was open and her door open too even if only a tiny crack. It was open so he waited, nobody left their door like that and went far or away at all, not on Sidojiwe E2.

He had come all this way down from the center of town at the post office on Main Street to Makokoba Township. He had to duck not once but twice a bucket of dirty bathwater being flung out into the street. It was nothing to wait another minute and catch his breath. He rested the bicycle against the hedge and fanned his scorched face using the letter held in his right hand, he bent down and rang the bell on the bicycle like an alarm.

He had been ringing the bell again and again and she had heard him, and not responded. Her mouth just dried up with the excitement and the bell confused her with its urgency and she needed just one quiet moment to think before moving forward, just a slice of silent time to pull her dress down, her thighs to slide off the small bench with its chipped base and cobwebs in all its four corners which she always omitted to clear. A pause, to nurse expectation to its highest pitch. She had waited for months for a response to her application. She could not believe the postman was looking for her, now, ringing his bell, now, at her, now, so that she could leave the room and enter its sweet sound and be set free, in a melody of her own, this instant. Before everything disappeared she unfroze her legs and pulled herself off the bench and let the kettle on the paraffin stove burn its water away while she stood outside and put wet thumbprints all over her new envelope before she could open it and let the finely folded paper with the emblem of the hospital on it slide out, before she could get back inside the house where she could smell the bottom of the kettle burning, she let it because she had to move outside again where there was enough light, and there, lighten her burden.

And now. She rushed out of the house and walked slowly along Sidojiwe E2 in order to gather her thought, her breath, her entire reason. With her eyes blind with fury, Phephelaphi saw Sidojiwe E2 for the first time. Papers were caught along the hedges which were covered with dust, the garbage bins were upturned and the children sat on their tops till the lids collapsed, abandoned tires lay filled with stagnant water, discarded tins littered the yards, women sat outside their stoops plaiting each other's hair, a radio blared a staccato tune to which a beggar danced, someone had painted ten different haircuts for men on the entire wall of the abandoned Baloos Store while nearby a barber sat and waited for customers to arrive. Meanwhile, all the hair he cut off fell into the ditch and lay unclaimed.

She saw young boys along the street. Young boys who were tantalized by the baritone love creeping down their throats and the stiffening of their chests, tantalized by the violent pulsing at the base of the neck, by the blood rushing to their minds, the hair under their armpits where a dark sweat made them different because it rose to their nostrils first thing in the morning and brought waves and waves of shame dripping down their thighs. With these ample signs their foreheads creased in a knowing, grown-up gaze as Phephelaphi went past, their heads leaned toward her and paused where she did, lifted in anticipation when she raised her arm and nursed her hurt. It was in their monotone gaze, lingering over each part of her blossoming self—as though the fruit was too high up the tree—but they could, and would, carry its scent for days, touch its ripening skin with their tender tongues. That was enough. They would bury its smooth taste on their palate for days even if the fruit was right at the top of the tree, the climb ill advised, the tree trunk barbed by thorns.

They pulled themselves back from where they dangled their legs upon the abandoned balcony at Baloos, where the embroidered wrought iron moulted handfuls of peeling paint. Past the metal milk cans. They leaped to safety and turned their attention back to earthly things. They sat on the ground and formed a circle, slapping a beat on their naked thighs, and it was stinging, louder and louder, their flesh and blood tight and resonant, their lips pursed in some silent tingling harmony, some knee-slapping wonderful song.

She saw the houses. They had been built mostly for bachelors, the women were not expected to follow their men to the city. The men smuggled what little comfort they could into these tiny shelters, and everything changed, otherwise what was a sunset for, and that closing darkness of the night, and the time before morning when everything throbs with a new sun, and you have to touch someone. How was all that to be dealt with and considered except for the closeness, the insideness of another being? They found what comfort was near and consoling.

The women had other ideas about their own fulfilment; not only did some of them arrive in the city independently of the men, they remained in these single shelters no matter what threat was advertised, they gave birth and raised children on the palms of their hands. Bicycles had either policemen or black women on them. The women rode into suburbs where from sunrise to sunset they kept, clothed, and fed white children from their own breasts. In the evening, they returned to Makokoba and cooked dried fish, or anything with a strong scent to it, stewed it into an irresistible succulence. They craved something possessing the hint of rivers or an expanse as wide and fascinating as the sea.

Phephelaphi had not known where exactly she was heading when she opened the door and entered Sidojiwe E2 but next she was standing, sitting, standing again with Deliwe, muttering incoherently and moving in circles on the porch, refusing to sit on the stoop, threatening to return with the tears still crushing her eyelids, the drums beating in her head like a storm, her temples burning, and everything about her frozen or dead, mumbling about seeing Fumbatha in a dream, and whispering, her voice like heated coal, about a woman called Emelda who had died in her arms, and mountains to climb even though there were none at all, complaining about trains and a vanishing sky, white uniforms for healing the sick, till Deliwe tired of trying to understand this taste of salt and sugar mixed together, so she rose in the middle of that fine afternoon and stopped dreaming of the syrup from her blooms, abandoned the lizards darting underneath the hedges, rose, decidedly, from her Southern Rhodesian beer crate and shoved Phephelaphi inside the house, sat her down on a stool, and gave her a glass of water. It was the glass that rescued her. A long glass with a blue tint to it which looked lovelier than sunlight and which, as Phephelaphi brought it to her lips, made her senses gather together like needles of incandescent light, as though her butterfly wings were closing on pollen, just touching, closed till a breeze

lifted and disturbed the pleat. Finally she was able to look up at Deliwe
and tell her all her shame. Deliwe listened carefully.

Deliwe who had been Getrude's friend.

Deliwe who knew Fumbatha.

Deliwe who had the pride of an eagle.

Deliwe who had eyes like scorpions.

Deliwe listened till the sky turned from blue to crimson light. Phephelaphi asked Deliwe if she could fill this same sky, once more, with
white clouds. Deliwe shook her head and carefully withdrew the tinted
glass from Phephelaphi's hands. Phephelaphi could barely breathe as
she staggered back along Sidojiwe E2. She heard her own door creak to
a close behind her.

fifteen

A week passed.

Phephelaphi heard the burst of voices, the children rushed past Sidojiwe E2 like a whirlwind. She heard the children as they rolled an old car tire and laughed as they chased and fell on one another, bursting with a singular eagerness, and they pushed the tire to and fro as though offering each other unique abandon, and their joy grew because something was rolling freely, their feet were animated with the same cheerful bliss and their arms ticklish with the absence of concern, ready to swing high at something half their height—a black tire full of motion whose energy they could not only outlast but rebuild. So they ran after it and rolled it again and again, and fell to the ground with the sheer gladness of it all, and the cycle of joy pulled them up, and made the earth shift and tilt backward while the houses shook and their mothers floated above the rooftops and the children laughed till their bodies hurt, their eyes full of tears, blind with the dust.

They lost the earth but gained the freedom of birds, so the bottle tops they had gathered preciously and importantly from the streets and outside the abandoned Baloos Store were briskly pushed into the hollow of the black and open tire where they would be forgotten for days. This safely done, the children forsook the world and looked at the tops of tall trees which seemed to wave and pass by. It was simple—they were breathless and all they could do was stare till everything settled along Sidojiwe E2.

The window was broken.

A large bottle of Vaseline partly blocked the large hole at the bottom of the small window. The Vaseline bottle was bright yellow. At the other end of the room Phephelaphi lay on the bed with half her body raised against the wall, and closed her eyes.

The bottle was green, then yellow. When she closed her eyes again she saw the deep yellow of the bottle. The green grew faint. Behind the window was the hedge, green, close. The broken glass had sharp edges. With her eyes she followed a jagged crack that climbed to the top of the remaining glass. This was morning.

She slid downward into the center of the bed and raised the coarse gray blanket over her breasts. She held the blanket against her chin. She held the blanket with both hands against her face. It had a bold red seam along the edges. Her elbows pushed and scraped against the blanket. She brought her knees forward, against the blanket, and this increased her warmth. She felt consoled and lay hidden in this curled position, then pressed and sank further into the hollow of the mattress, which flattened and reached the cold cement floor.

She wanted an opportunity to be a different woman and 1948 was a

year when hope opened like a bright sky and an educated black woman
could do more. The offer was there and it made her breathless just to
imagine being anything else other than what she was. It was nothing she
knew but she wanted it, missed the future somehow. She was nothing
now. She was not anything that she could feel. She wanted to be something with an outline, and even though she was not sure what she
meant, she wanted some respect, some dignity, some balance and power
of her own. Finding herself. Her passion was secret and undisclosed.
Yet, it could change something. Fumbatha would never understand so
she said nothing to him.

In the fear which embraced her for that entire week Phephelaphi
had learned that everything else between a man and a woman could be
forgotten; the caress, the touch, their lips searching, and the belonging
which made each movement tempting, their mingling necessary. This
could be forgotten. Portions of their voices. This was passing. It was
possible to part, to turn and walk away even after he had made and unmade her. She wanted more. A part of her hardened against him. He
had now intruded on her dream.

She brought the blanket closer to her face and over her mouth. She
could smell the rough fabric and held it even closer to her face. The
touch and the smell of the material repelled her. She brought the blanket closer. Her eyelids closing. Nearer. She tightened her grip over the
edge of the blanket. The thread showed like streaks of blood between
her fingers.

The window had been broken last week when someone had thrown
a large stone into the house and nearly killed her. Two men were quar-
reling in the middle of Sidojiwe E2 and she had heard them. One of
them threatened with a knife, the other picked the large stone. It landed
on the bed where she had been sleeping. Phephelaphi wished the stone
had killed her.

Instead, she remained with her anger and anxiety. She took the stone and placed it under the bed. She spent many days while Fumbatha was away sleeping on the bed, looking through the window at the figures passing on the other side of the green hedge, thinking of the child. Phephelaphi heard the sound of a bicycle moving past and saw a hand raise a hat up into the air and wave in slow circles—a black hat, while the figure to whom it belonged remained hidden beneath the hedge, underneath the window. To see the man on the bicycle she would have to rise from the bed and approach the window which was located some distance from the floor. Instead the hand and the hat rode past. The women standing on the other side of the street called out a greeting. The hat had a single tall feather, white, tucked along its black brim.

She wanted a silence in which she could separate each of her thoughts. Then a voice selling apples shattered her sleep. She heard it grow fainter and fainter as though the faintness was something failing inside her. The voice continued to call, repeatedly, inside her. It spread like a ripple and she thought again that the power to bring it to a pitch was hers. It was a beseeching call and this confused her emotion and she wanted to awaken the voice and make it louder, then she could hear all the search in it that surely could be awakened. It was impossible to accomplish anything from where she lay, a partial witness to every complete reality. She must see the seller. If she did this, she would have changed all the voices inside her. This involved rising to her feet and going to the window. She continued to lie down and chose to find a gap of time in which her thought would be clear, her idea uninterrupted. Sidojiwe E2 was suddenly the noisiest street she could imagine. She strove for that fraction of time that would belong to her.

A fragment is also a life, it is how all of life is lived, in patches. She chose other distractions. Phephelaphi curled her arm over the edge of the bed and reached for the stone which had fallen through the window.

She had shoved it there. She remembered it there. When her fingers touched its smooth side she turned over the bed to her side and her knees collapsed as she rolled over to bring her right arm back to her stomach, with the weight in her hands. Her feet touched the cold metal frame on the bottom end of the bed. She raised her arms and breathed deeply. The blanket rested beneath her breasts and she tucked its edges beneath her body to warm herself. She wore nothing. She thought deeply about the child.

It was better to hold memory in your hands. Otherwise whatever was not physical disappeared. In the safety of touch, memory had a shape she could conjure without panic. It was reachable. She had secured something solid that could help conviction. Phephelaphi questioned each event because it had passed. She fought against this vanishing with a multitude of objects. The room was full of her memories. Each separate agony distinctly shaped; a hair comb, a spoon, a shoe. She abhorred what was elusive and could not be held up to the tongue to be tasted or to the fingers to be felt.

To have. The act of possession. The act of bringing the senses forward and discovering sound was important, like holding something in the hand, a broken heel, the edges of a torn mattress, an empty green bottle. And yet, this feeling of impending loss was too tangible. This longing, that misery, this pressure, that neglect, this distress, that relief, this yearning, that command. Fumbatha could no longer be part of her dream.

Phephelaphi pulled the stone toward her and held it. It had not been broken though it had been flung through the window and straight on to the opposite wall, then back to the bed where she lay. Only one edge of it was chipped. The events she remembered were true. Here was the object; and the time. Alongside it the beating of her heart, bare feet touching the cold ground, the black rubber band tied tight and close around the broom is rubbing against her palm, her thumb digs into this fold of grass, and her arm moves in brief quick strokes over the floor. She is frightened. She hears the broom on broken glass scraping upon the floor. She brings the shards of glass into a neat pile which she slides and pushes safely against the wall. She places the small grass broom over the pile and waits for morning. For light. She needs to see what has occurred.

She had picked the stone from the bed where it had fallen and carefully turned it in her hand. Not a single sound followed the event except her own deep inhalation swallowed by the breaking glass, and she wondered where the men had vanished to. She heard her own surprised shout mingle with the glass and meet the floor. Then a silence so undisturbed it made her disbelieve the evidence—the glass piled to the corner of the room. The darkness made her doubt each detail. A portion of her mind rejected the broken glass, as in a way it rejected the child she was expecting. She denied her own existence and moved, like a shadow, back to the window. She heard nothing. No voice called. Nothing shouted. No one moved.

Something raced toward her, an emotion with no shape that she recognized. It was a current of grief and regret larger than her own mind and stronger and more decided. The emptiness had decided all there was to decide about her insignificance and her lack of wisdom and she was nothing but a shallow substance. There was evidence of her lack. She was nothing. How could she love her own elbows and turn her arm like a rope, the way her mother did? She was nothing under the sky. In her mind she saw a cloth tossing and swaying. Even though this was all in her mind she felt the same cool breeze that was blowing the cloth touch her face. She was much less than a thin fabric tearing in the wind. What was she? She did nothing but remain mute and peaceful and could not be absorbed by this thin fabric which knew so much more than she did because it had witnessed each of her actions before she performed them.

In the instant that realization again crept forward and grasped her, she rose from the bed quickly and reached for a packet of Lion matches, not sure which thought was most dominant in her mind, the child or the broken window. A scrape against the box and she lit the match. The match lasting briefly as it starts to burn a tiny blue flame which rose to the tip of her fingers and which she moved to the cup where she dipped her hand and lit the candle.

She had to nurse the candle to bring it alive as the wick was folded and had dried into the hollow at the top. She kept the match dipped into the groove till the candle melted and she could raise the small thread and pass the flame to it. She coaxed the flame as the match shortened and the light reached for her skin—between her thumb and forefinger. The flame was blue and bright. Focusing on lighting the candle, she had almost forgotten why she had awakened, and why it was necessary to have light. This action alone was true; her fingers, the match, the candle in the cup, the darkness.

The darkness was whole. The light soft. Then the light grew whole, the darkness soft. In the whirring of the dark and in the ringlet of fear that rose above her she slipped to the floor and crouched near the cup and the candle, her elbows hit the wall above which was the broken window, above which was the light, above those strange tall trees, the red roofs, the telegraph wires, above which was the moon and the stars, above which was her mounting sorrow, her desperate panic, and the child.

Finally the light made a round glowing circle above the cup. Phephelaphi hung in that light and watched the candle grow into the rim, till her lips shone above this flaring circle. The light poured out of the cup and showed the entire length of her arms, the deep groove upon her forehead, and her eyes bright. Her effort calm. The darkness was whole, the light wholesome.

She swept the glass in the dark. The candle burned inside the metal cup. She picked the cup and brought it searchingly to the different corners of the room then placed it on the floor. She swept the floor clean and ran her palm over it to feel that it was now smooth and clean, without broken glass. She abandoned the broom and walked to the opposite end of the room where she rolled the stone under the bed.

s i x t e e n

No. No suspicion of falling and therefore no desire to lay a grip on something solid or to lean on someone, somewhere. No need for anything as stiff as a will. But again, no lightness either. The type of weightlessness that comes with looking down a steep descent. This alone would have helped with flight or merely drawing the shoulders forward and the knees to a resolution. Feeling the weight of the top of tall trees—their lush green, their wave and pause. Just a pure longing for land that heaves and swells up to the sky, forming wide hills whose backs hold basins filled with a calm essence, begetting grass, singing insects and trees, land that pauses, then listens as a leaf drops, as a raindrop drops, and vanishes.

Instead, in this flat expanse arms are free and not groping toward another truth, and the eyes press directly upon the ground. The body is free. It is alone. Not disturbed. The ground near and naked, you can smell its absence of weight. The body is only a feather held upright, pinned down to the ground and poised to fall from the slightest whisper. It is suspended, ready to collapse when a shadow falls. You are on the ground with nothing to measure the distance between the tip of one finger and the top of the shoulder when the arm is held out, nothing to secure height, or to know the pace of footsteps, to measure the tremors of distrust or of a cruel inhalation.

There is no support for the spine. The people look tiny and safe, move like quills in this slim and lit space between the sky and the ground. The pounding of the heart, the solitary whisper, the agony of temptation—nothing to examine these. A broad green leaf held across the hand would have helped to cure tragedy, a way of measuring experience—the ambiguous, the futile, and the magnificent. A broad green leaf. None of this. Thorns break boldly from every shrub. Gray and silver and dry. Stark and perfectly still.

And courage, how is that to be measured without the firm bark of a tree somewhere about, or at least, something soft as the surface of a lake. A reflection. Nothing to consider tenderness. Where is good fortune to be found without the top of hills, the smooth fall into some valley, some inviting groove of the earth, some fabulous rapture so that at least one feels older than spite, swings away from fate and folly?

Land with movement. A varied motion of the horizon where the eyes swing from hill to valley, turn from the tops of trees back to the valley—this is a movement necessary for comfort. There is none of this.

The land is bare and sparse with dots of short bush. Here, a thorn. Here, a bird. Just dots of living across this stretching flat land. Then further, fields and fields of dry waving grass, and no trees. On the other side, beyond the stunted bushes, is Makokoba, within it is Sidojiwe E2, Jukwa Road, Bambanani, L Road, D Square, and Banda Road, and many more. A black location. The houses tiny shelters, like the shrubs. Around them, tall trees introduced one by one after each row of houses, standing on guard against an anticipated accident, some incident of fracture, like breaking bone. In each street dream rubs against dream. Near and close.

Sturdy thorns with dry and cracking bark, and long narrow fingers, firm, with a color of tan like darkened glass.

Phephelaphi has no fear as the sky falls over her forehead with flickers of lost desire, no fear, only the separate grains of sand under her feet; and an entire day.

Push. She has pushed it in. Sharp and piercing. No fear. No excitement. This must be. In and out of a watery sac. Slowly she receives it as though this motion will provide an ecstatic release. Her hand is steady inside her body. Her own hand inserting an irreversible harm. Her right arm is supported by the inside of her thigh which is carefully raised from the ground. At the wrist, her hand turns sharply inward, as though broken. Her hand moves and beats in rapid motions. She keeps her head on the ground, away from her thighs. Her left leg is lowered on the ground and stretched out. Her hand slips past her left thigh. She is full of tension. Her fingers hold firm at each frantic pierce. The land is still. From a distance, she is only a mark on the ground.

Her body accepts each of her motions, her legs spread open, wider, both knees now raised higher and higher into the forever light of day, listening for the tremor she anticipates, and she feels it, beginning with the lukewarm warmth along her arm, hardly felt, like water left uncovered under the sun now spilling over, a vessel filled to the brim, the lukewarm warmth trickling down, then pouring, sinking, excruciating. A hurt lingers. Wave after wave and the lukewarm warmth is thickening and brave. It is her own vessel filled to capacity. It is herself, her own agony spilling over some fine limit of becoming which she has ceased suddenly to understand, too light and too heavy. It is she. She embraces it, braces for the tearing. Her body breaks like decayed wood. Deep in the near deep of her, so close it is so deep and near in the same instant. She dares not look at her own harm. It is too near and new.

The pain is more than she imagines. It is cutting. She holds it in her elbows which she pushes into the ground, behind her. She has to place the pain somewhere away from her own body. Somewhere else. But there is nowhere to hide anything. There is no shelter. Only her fingers merge with the agony of her release. Her right hand closes. She has to accept her own pain in order to believe it, to live in it, to know its true and false nuances, for she desires desperately what is beyond the pain. She seeks something neutral and unthought. Just to be. Some kind of living but not this. To reach that fine plateau, this pain is a boulder she must defeat, and so she surrenders her cry to it, her time to it, and her joy too. She remembers her joy. She longs for some hill, some shape for her eyes to move over before she can touch the sky. She longs for the long branch of a tree just waiting for birds to perch on it, something to rid the anxiety. There is no relief. Instead the pain sharpens and pulls at her. It burns, bottomless burning, beyond any action she might perform to reverse it. It whirls and stirs through her entire body and she is lightning. A streak of heat.

She slips away, a swimmer in noiseless water, through something soft and liquid which surrounds her entire body and it is as though she has forgotten everything, where she has been and what has been. An eternity passes, a gap of time she is not aware of, except this calm, this not being part of anything at all, not her body, not the sky above her, not the not-here tree which she imagines, not even the not-hereness with hills to be imagined, the emptiness and none being. Not here. Instead, a quiet stretch of time where she is not. Not being. The soft liquid is now full of light. Phephelaphi.

Her back is on the ground and her knees tremble. Her shoulders are half buried in the abundant and soft soil. Her head curls to the left and leaves her face resting over her left shoulder. Her eyes waiting. Tears squeeze through her tightly closed eyes tracing every intense furrow and each line of dismay. One half of her lower lip is caught between her teeth. Held tightly against surrender. She presses her face down further onto her shoulder till her head is buried in the firm warmth of the sun, and her hair is the color of sand. Changed, absorbed, her whole form is a wooden mask floating in the rapid sand. Drop after drop the land welcomes her tears like rain.

She is lightning, burning like it. She is fire and flame. She is light. Then in her grief she clutches something as dead as a root. She fastens her grip over this dead substance which promises no anchor. No promises to rescue and heal. Hope fades after hope. Slowly, her hold loosens and she slips again further into the soft lightness of a liquid stream. Her own open legs. Her body dissolves in the truest substance of pain. She has to move out of the ground but her movements are tortured. She turns her face back toward her body and relaxes her elbows. Her neck is raised forward, searching, rotating back to her left for a missed detail. Ahead, she finds her knees pulled up, and apart. Behind there is a stretch of empty land and then the thorn bush.

The thorn bush from where she had earlier retrieved the longest and strongest needle she could find. This bush is now bright with dots of red. The red surprises her and fills her eyes because it was not there before. Perhaps she is just too tired. She looks cautiously again through the bush which is now covered with red blooms. There are red blooms. She accepts this as her failure to remember where she is, and what has been. Then, a sudden loud shudder and escape, lifting into the sky is a shrill breaking chorus, then she realizes that these veering red dots are the beaks of dozens of gray birds which have been resting within the thorns. The birds fly off in scattering cries. Their sound swells toward her. A dotted shadow spreads overhead leaving a multitude of beating wings in meandering layers. The red drops whirl past her body and reel into the back of her mind.

Phephelaphi shifts her skirt upward and over the middle of her shivering and moist back. The skirt is tight. She twists the skirt to one end and she can feel the thick band rubbing against her skin, resisting her motion. A black button falls. A memory falls. The button has fallen from her blouse along the front. It lies half buried below her left elbow. The zipper scrapes her back as she twists her skirt to one side. She turns and turns it till her left finger can reach the zipper and pull it down.

The band loosens, the skirt wider. The skirt moves easily and she can proceed to pull it in one direction. She pushes her body forward in order to free the rest of her cloth. She pulls the pleats of the skirt together into a bundle that she tucks firmly and safely under her. She protects her dress. The cold metal of the zipper is pulled over her navel. Her body is almost naked. Except for the blouse. Along the open front the button is gone. She is naked except for the weight of her own suffering, the weight of courage.

The land is dry. The rain is too far, too long ago. The sand is loose and shifts beneath her elbows like a tired breeze. Her elbows are buried in the sand. Her heels dig down. Her anxiety penetrates the ground. Too close, an unbearable sudden ache, and way too far. Hidden and tearing. Deeper. Deeper. And the lukewarm warmth becomes a solid. Thicker and immediate. It is hard. It slides and shifts like handfuls of saliva. It is too thick for saliva and too heavy to gather all of it only with her mind, the pain and touch of it is too extraordinary, too pure.

For a brief time the sky has hills in it, the sky has many hills in it.

She can see the drop of the valley and the basins with the same calmness that is inside her own body. A feeling, clean and ordered, floods her waiting body. She accepts it even as it recedes and the tears begin to well unbidden, and the pain climbs up her back and pulls her to a hidden place and her eyes are closed against the bright light. The valley is still held in her eyes so she can find a small place to hide while she watches hills fold onto hills and cast protective shadows into every slice of her pain.

The stars are all carried in our eyes, this is why we are alone. We are yet to be born. Some of us are never to be born. To be born is chance and good fortune, and to survive into tomorrow, sheer motive and interest. She was not interested.

She thinks of something else altogether while the child pulls away from her and finds the sky so low it graces her knees which are weak and folding. The hills have disappeared and are gone. They have been flattened to the ground by the simple drop of her eyelids. In a mixture of laughter and tears she sees again the crimson beaks, red scratches across an entire blue sky. They land with silent wings back on the thorn bush, waving a shadow past her body like a fleeting breeze. All sound is stilled under the rise and rhythm of these wings. The birds merge with the dull thorns. Beautiful red blooms embrace, once more, the bush. Indeed, she can smell the pollen and see the bees. She laughs a lone woman's mad quiet laugh, rich with fateful recognition and regretful desire. From a distance, her laugh is only a mark on the ground.

Her thighs tremble but her body is buried far from the shelter of the bushes which are bare of leaves and offer no relief. She buries her head within the fold of her right arm, above her elbow. She has to close her eyes and fold her arms to support this last seeping of desire. Strong wave after wave is released like a flood breaking over the bank of the river, discovering a new shore where water has not been. She is at the bottom of the river but it is dry there. She is untouched by the flood tearing the riverbed from shore to shore. The river is a pounding and deafening omniscience. This is not water but a liquid wind—a pool of fire in which she burns without pause. Nothing has been born. Nothing has been born at all. Nothing has been taken away.

Time closes her eyes and then, slowly, gathers an undiscovered strength that propels her forward like a petal carried in a current of wind. Her fingers are slippery. Her skin burns. Time endures each rupture as though a flower were blooming or a leaf were being cleansed.

The thorns and the red petals wait together. She is standing on shaky legs near the bush weaving a cradle out of thorn. Her fingers bleed as she breaks each small branch, each tiny wing of shrub. The skin on her hands tears. She leaves the delicate blooms intact. She weaves a nest, a coarse cradle of thorn which she offers to the ground near her feet where a smooth agony flows. The cradle holds her flowing blood like a sieve. The gray and smooth sharpness of each thorn locks bravely into another and rests beneath her body, a tight nest, above it is the stretch of her body and its shiver toward light, beneath her the child, not yet, is released.

Falling on a basket of thorns, on the separate sand, each grain pushing away from the other, not touching, not knowing, not belonging. Arrows of light, not seeming to be from a single place but passing through her whole body, as though she is a transparent membrane coating the inside shell of an egg.

She feels the heat on the inside of her arm, over her elbow, the hidden curve of her foot and knows she is nowhere nearer those petals than here. She is on this ground with a heavy forehead licked with pain, with sweat dripping behind her ears. Her pain knows no bounds. She is on the ground struggling against a fierce fear and surrender.

She pulls the nylon petticoat held past her waist, under the skirt.

She pulls it down, toward her knees and over her feet. When she has removed it she brings the nylon cloth to her face and wipes her forehead. The cloth simply slips over her and falls to the ground beside her but she repeatedly picks it and replaces it on her forehead. She holds the cloth down though her hands are shaking and soaked. She presses hard and wipes her forehead, again and again. When she is done her face is dry to breaking.

Nothing in her is consoled, nothing concealed. She clears her forehead. The cloth, wet and spreading the wetness through her fingers, has become more slippery, now filled with the warmth of her body. She carries this warmth across her stomach. As she proceeds, she feels the wet fabric over her. She reaches down and tucks the nylon petticoat between her thighs.

The skirt is a hard mass underneath her, between her alarming hurt and the ground. Her left arm folds over her body and finds the lump of cloth, and brings it up to her front. Her entire left side is now resting directly on the ground, and immediately, she understands that this crushed cloth, though a hardness that has brought a continuous ache to her side, has become an anchor. An anchoring ache. She holds this unraveling cloth across her body as she attempts to rise from the ground with the petticoat and the warmth wedged securely between her legs.

The land, soft pliant sifting soil, carries her entire shape on it. She sees the place where she has been buried when she lifts her body forward from the ground and offers the blood to her petticoat. The blood soaks into the fabric and she folds her right hand and gathers, with the thin nylon fabric, the lukewarm warmth which is no longer her own.

Steady and steadier. She receives each motion of her body and the liquid spreads over her arm, over the sliding nylon in her fingers, and the unborn child too small to be a child, just a mingling within the nylon, something viscous and impolite amid the lace spreading along the hem, and the elastic gathering the nylon into pretty pink frills that glisten, shimmer, cupped in her hand. She closes her hand secretly.

The ground is soft and she moves it, shifts it easily with her fingers, handfuls of soil burning with the scent of the sun, and easy, easy grains of sand. The grains turn freely and bright with daylight. Between each grain the soil is a fine brown powder, crushed to a sacred lightness. Her fingers are wet, so the grains of sand paste along the wetness and climb over her quiet arm. She gathers this abundant soil rapidly and its motions are graceful and easy like a greeting. Suddenly, beneath the softness of the soil, is the hard ground. A black hard helmet, compact, and she fails to hollow or break it.

Is. Is. Is. This soil just is. It does not move. No kindness to it. It is a violent quiet. A plain roof sealing the bottom of the earth. Water could not dissolve its rigid hold, its stiff will. She burrows like certain kinds of animals which fear prey and have nowhere to hide, whose coats are too visible, whose odor, though meant to defend them, leaves a trail too apparent to be ignored. Their desperation, their movements, tell an entire distrust. The ground is rock and resists each of her attempts to open it with her desperate hands.

Only the soft soil slides to one side, piles over, slides and piles over. The soft soil forms a mound, a bowl for her warm tears which have not yet fallen. It is so dry and fine that when she presses it together it holds together like a batter. Yet the slightest wind frees it and it turns into air. But inside it is even drier land, intense like a repeated dream, tight and holding together. It is darker, and its triumph matches something inside the roof of her head where there is a constant burning. Everything that burns soon turns to ash. She digs beyond this core, the soil is smooth, charitable, full of pardon. It has turned into ash. She takes this soil into the bowl of her knitted fingers and raises it up, above her head, higher, separates it, and it falls like a sweet memory to the ground.

She is thinking of her thirst, and wondering how long it will be before she can taste water. In her longing is the pliant soil, like loam, and the taste of water. She longs for simple truths; a morning with just the rising sun and its caress of the earth, just that. She laughs at her longing of something else beginning, something harmless like sunrise, something she need not measure against her own body. Out there, tantalizing, far off in the horizon. Yes, a sunrise with a wild tumult like red dust. That is it. Familiar and free. A liquid ferment.

A lack of water. Water brings things together. Two stones in a pool of water become one, but in the air each is proud and alone. Two sticks, two eyes that belong to the face of a child. When a plant dries, it bears the indifference of stone. Often, it burns. It is light like dust.

She is in dry land. Waiting in an eternity. She burrows the ground, her tongue held between her teeth in surprise. Her focus held against a gentle softness ready to yield such an impenetrable wall. A lulling sandy soil, an impassive ground.

The thorns match the sharp edge of the horizon. Here, both morning and day offer the same slicing circle of sky and hard earth. Unless there is some other object in sight, turning the body around means nothing crucial, no change but the same sight over the shoulder, unless of course you know something about clouds, their shape and weight which meets the eye, the water in them, or, most of the time, the water not in them. If there is water you can sniff it from the cloud like pollen. Changing direction means something else entirely, maybe about living, certainly not the notion of shoulders realigned against the trunk of a tree, or a boulder, or a river, or hope.

When the sky is a solid unforgiving blue all round, then one searches for the tiny spray of whispered sentences twisting in and out of the sky. This distant dance above is something as noticeable as a faint breeze passing over a mound of feathers. A disturbance which does not change the absolute contours of the object but its emotion. It is a suggestion which, like the naive breathing of a child released on a grain of rice, frees the broken shell.

Sometimes there are thin and narrow pestles wavering, suspended, and they look like anthills in the sky. And the whole bowl of sky looks as though it has hills floating in it. There are dark hills with white smoke swirling over them. Then rocks hanging on the borders of smaller rocks, over and over, and touching the sky on all sides of its horizon. Nothing tumbling, just some curved reality. This is dryness, not water.

There is a crack, like thin and dry twigs; the break of a branch.

The smoothness of her thighs is beautiful like a remembered scent which carries one toward another moment which is separate, not joined by water. This is a safe place. The passing of this moment is brief. The touch along her left thigh holds like a prolonged sigh.

The sky is low and lights everything with its glow. The grains of sand are a silver glitter like drops of dew. The air cools to a crisp freshness and she feels it over her forehead, the tiny breeze growing and fanning her eyes. She closes her eyes and listens to her skin cool to mildness. Her knees turn cold. Each burden vanishes with the strength gathering in her knees and she knows she can walk and find shelter of her own.

The heart beating is hers, her arms, and she is she. She has emerged out of a cracked shell. There is a soothing emptiness in this canopy of sky. She has endured the willed loss of her child. Willed, not unexpected. Expected, not unwilled. The dried blood over her thighs, between her fingers, her head spinning and heavy, the dry ground, hollowed and free.

This.

Each moment is hers and she recalls each detail with clarity even while she is still living it, living in it, part of it, and parting from it. Rising, she must remember. The soil around her moulded like clay. Dark with the blood that is hers. Her petticoat missing, buried under a crust of dry ground. Her skirt falling down from her waist to her knees. The fabric flaring its folded seams from where the sand showers down from its folds to her feet. The hem swings over her skin. The skirt is bright yellow and covers her knees.

When she pulls the zipper along the skirt it is already broken. She pulls the cloth and tucks the button at the top of the zipper firmly into the seam on the opposite side, along the band, and she allows the blouse to fall untidily over the skirt. The material is wrinkled. This too she remembers. The mess and untidy chaos. This whole action had been about tidying up. Ordering the disorder. Instead, her fingers are torn and bleeding. Her blouse is open at the top where the button has fallen. She looks behind her and to the ground, where her elbow has been. The button has disappeared and she knows it is futile to search for it.

The remaining thread hangs on the fabric where the button had been secured. Already she plans to move the last button on the blouse to the top of the garment. This action will change how she feels, now, in the midst of her confusion. Her breasts are naked. Her nipples are tender as they rub against the cloth, as though scalded, and in the groove where her breasts meet she is touched with the sun's coolest rays.

She spreads smooth soil over the dotted spots which are going round and round on the ground where an animal, wounded, has performed a lonely rite. She spreads the clear sand cleanly over the marks. In the grave grasp of her own agony, in her riotous release, she pours handful and handful. The finest soil blows away, while the heaviest grains fall quickly downward. The finest soil blinds.

Phephelaphi closes her eyes and pours her sorrow down. She adds more and more of the soil till she has formed a high mound around her and then she collapses to the ground. She has built a solid mound of earth smooth like ash. Then she rests. Her gain restored.

A firmament of despair. Whoever has to be buried in this land is placed in the lightest soil there is, so light ants can carry it, paste it with saliva, and build structures higher than trees.

seventeen

Time expands like the banks of a river during a flood.

Whole weeks pass before Fumbatha returns. She is intense with waiting though grateful for his absence. Each day she feels recovered. Phephelaphi walks in a stupor, unable to bury her pain; not clear if she has parted from death or life. Folded into two halves, one part of her is dead, the other living. Not knowing which is the stronger; her pain involves this struggle. Awake, she is consumed by a strong temptation to tell a stranger that her life has ended. A stranger would gather the details and toss them to the wind.

Fear dissolves into anguish. She recalls the bicycle bell which had brought her a letter. A song lights her lips but she has no words for it. She tries again. No words, just their shape, a frantic bell, salt over her tongue. The gathered dust. The lost tune. The nails digging into palms soft like crumbling wood.

She hears the crack of the asbestos as the roof pulls and contracts above her: a sound as of bones folding. Her body moves from intense heat to cold and a landscape she barely recognizes rises to the surface and leaves her disbelieving. A blank patch exists where fear has been; something has vanished. The search is crucial. She stumbles and falls. No shoes. It is winter in mid-June. Her foot hooks against a sheet of metal left outside the grounds at United School. Blood on her writing pad spreading from her fingers; she has wiped clean her injured foot with her bare hands.

An obstacle whichever direction her mind opens. Something else, larger and solid, has cast a terrible shadow into her being, split her mind into irreconcilable parts, breaks her memory into fragments. This shadow has swallowed every other detail, her lonesome search, and she wonders therefore, why she still fails to close her eyes and sleep, and forget the fine dust sucking at her throat, hindering her.

The room is so small that trying to hide a thought is a doomed ambition. Phephelaphi lifts herself up. She rises to the surface feeling like a stream of light, as though she has not eaten for days, wave after wave. She takes a wet cloth, bends down, and wipes the drops of blood which go round the room. Her arm moves quickly, back and forth. She wants to recover before Fumbatha returns into the hidden truth of her actions. She waits.

It is Zandile she remembers most. She closes her eyes painfully and sees Zandile, her hand upon her waist, her back leaning against the wardrobe. She recalls how Zandile takes her aside and offers her the dress she had worn back in the 1920s. Zandile checks first to see if Boyidi can hear her secret and anxious whispers, then she turns toward Phephelaphi, who looks at this new Zandile in amazement, this more-than-caring Zandile who wants to offer her all that is treasured in her past, who makes it seem that her friendship with Getrude is a phenomenal virtue which redeems her in every way, but that it is up to Phephelaphi to keep that friendship true, to make its innocence linger.

Phephelaphi refuses the dress. She has already concluded that Zandile is like a spider; she wants her caught in a web. When she refuses, Zandile's eyes glitter; she is not a woman who tolerates rejection. Now she speaks to Phephelaphi as though she no longer cares, her tone greedy and mocking, as though she has not been trying, a short while ago, to offer her a gift. "You are not a man, Phephelaphi. What are you going to do in Makokoba without being a man? Do you not know that a woman only has a moment in which to live her whole life? In it she must choose what belongs to her and what does not. No one can verify her claim except time. Makokoba is unkind to women like you who pretend to be butterflies that can land on any blossom they choose."

Zandile claims she knows Getrude as well as she knows her own shadow. "I built my own house in Makokoba not out of asbestos sheets, but out of brick and cement. It is one room, but it is my own solid shelter," Zandile says. She reminds Phephelaphi. About this. About that. About her own fierce hurt.

Phephelaphi waits for Fumbatha to return.

Fumbatha feels a deep loss even as he leaves Phephelaphi. It is not a fear of finding her gone which preoccupies him, it is that she has closed him out. He feels the pain of their separation as though she has rejected him with entire words. The last two nights with her had been the most difficult. He wants to ask why.

He leaves with relief that he has somewhere else to go. He can consider each of her silences; a silhouette he cannot define. He watches her disappear into the gulf between them as though she has dived into a river. She hears nothing of what he says. He stores his questions away. He leaves.

He does not hurry back. He remembers. Phephelaphi lowering herself into the bed, sinking beside him, pressing herself to him. Her body warm, her eyes empty of desire, yet she manages to rouse him, to bring him to her. She slides her hand over his back, with the other she brings his head gently down. A sharp intake of breath as she receives him, and he pauses, withdraws, but she holds him down, then receives him again. She holds him tightly between her thighs. She fears each nearness, as though he brings her harm. Fumbatha wonders if she has met another man during his absence but such a thought terrifies him and he brushes it quickly aside. She has been weeping. The truth of this is too difficult for him to absolve.

He wants to show her that her rejection does nothing to destroy his need for her. He needs her even if she stands apart and watches him. Does she not know the true measure of time between them; that what time they have already spent together is an eternity. Does she not know the true measure of distance between them; that he can touch her without lifting any of his fingers. The true measure of memory; her body embraced in water. The true measure of abandon; only she could bear his children, only then would he dream new dreams and all the children be saved from drowning. The true measure of escape; both her arms waiting. Death; the lack of her refuge?

Phephelaphi says nothing about the source of her troubles.

On the day he is to leave again she acts as though she has forgotten who he is, dimly aware of his presence. He lingers simply to prove his resolve of the earlier evening that loving her is something outside her body, something not connected to her choices to give, to receive, to share. He feels anxiety brush inside him like a cold shadow. This time he does not try to move from her but continues with each of his motions, and then releases her.

He is in the river with her, holding his breath the way she has said he should. He can survive even if she closes him out. He holds his breath for the longest time that he can find and pays tribute to an eternity. Fumbatha tries to recall, between each breath and motion of his shoulders, each of Phephelaphi's silences, the one truest thing a woman had told him.

Phephelaphi says nothing to place his fears at bay. That night he dreams of a lake of light and sees his father drown. In the morning he slides quickly out of the bed and leaves the room before she opens her eyes and watches him with that now familiar blank stare which says he is a stranger to her and that the only thing she knows about him is his name. He cannot bear it. How can he ask for the name of his father and survive? How can he ask what is hidden when the most enduring truth is not always spoken with words?

The morning is dark with a soft glow over the rooftops as he walks all the way down Sidojiwe E2. As he passes on the other side of Deliwe's flamboyant thorn bushes, Fumbatha sees that Deliwe's door is partly open and wonders quietly what kind of woman invites, without regret or burden, and at whatever time of day it was, at whatever cost, every infinite sorrow going past her doorway.

Fumbatha walks faster into the welcoming distance. As he moves on he notices that the remarkable difference on Sidojiwe E2 at that time of day is not the degree of light over the roofs and hedges, but the absolute darkness that exists merely because there are no children playing. The children, encased in sleep and dream, are truly missing and Sidojiwe E2 is not the street he knows. He continues in poignant resignation.

He wishes to have delayed his departure and managed to carry away with him the echo of a child's pattering feet. Their ringing voices which follow him like a multitude of rays.

eighteen

He knew it.

How or when she had no idea. Two months before her June
Intake she knew he knew that she had been expecting their child.
He knew it, for sure. It was the way he did things in a manner
which reminded her more and more of how he used to do things,
with an attention which had her as the center of it; included her,
absorbed her, considered her first, in each of his movements. It
was the absence of this which made her know that he knew even
if he did not say that he did. It was not the manner he looked at
her but that he ceased, altogether, to see her. He held her at a distance and peeled her arm off his back before morning. She noticed. The way he offered her only one word at a time. Pebbles
that are words. He forgot things. He forgot things she liked and

stopped whistling her favorite song and let his overalls hang around his waist and brought its two arms together and tied them down. He preferred this to her arms. He sat like that with his white vest sticking to his skin because the afternoon was so hot but he refused to let her open the door, not even its top half. He wanted the door kept closed and the world unobserved.

He had fixed the broken window. He had spent all of two days fixing it. He did not ask who had broken it or how but brought a new sheet of glass. He cut it carefully to size, grinding away at the edges and measuring carefully, glass, pane, back to glass, making sure nothing cracked where he did not want it to. He laid the entire sheet on top of a pile of newspapers. His knuckles stood out as he held it firmly down and worked his way around it. Cautious and delicate he gathered each move, held his breath as though the shattering of glass would cost a life. He dug his teeth into his lower lip. He knew.

She wondered but dared not ask. She wanted the two months to pass, quickly, so that she could move into the hospital hostel and start her training and be finished by the end of 1950, but while thinking of that and avoiding his eyes and tolerating his angry touch, she wondered how he knew, and when. The glass on the window held his fingerprints all over it. She wanted to clean the glass, but instead let it remain like that for days. She did not want to interfere with anything he had done. She dared not provoke him. They now lived in a stunning, shattering silence. She could not ask him the questions she wanted answered, so she let it be. If he could not talk about it she would not, but at the back of her mind she wanted desperately to know about his knowing, the extent and breadth of it, and if he too was holding his breath down like she was.

He spent time away even when she knew he had not gone to work. He just disappeared. Often. It bothered her but she dared not ask. He came back changed, able to look at her, smiling as though he wanted to give her a gift but she knew it was scorn and anger not love. Perhaps some combination of all those, but nothing straight and certain anymore, and she thought it would help if she knew how he could have known when she had been so alone in it all, so desperate in her escape. He held it against her. He said nothing, and this was worse than his angry words. His simmering silence. She sought the how, and the when, and found none. She started hoping she was mistaken, her fear burned into a low harmless flame, and she drew him close. She wanted to forget everything which had happened. If she touched his sinewy hips, his straight arm, his narrow back, she would forget. She drew him closer than she ever had. She wanted to be buried in him and forget the hard soil which had broken her fingers. Her longing was deep. She decided he did not know, that it was her fear which absorbed her and made it seem that he knew.

And then it was her turn to know something unsaid. When it happened, her body sank into the bottomless earth with its unsupportable anguish, something in the way a man pulls you toward him and pins you down, the pace of it, the hurry or delay shows you where he has been, and that his body has known, already, before reaching yours, some other woman's smiling arms, some thighs, some sweetness somewhere, not here. This knowing without being told is agony. Your eyelids and every part of your body heats up or freezes and then a desperate churning comes and goes, comes and goes, deep in your stomach where your desire suddenly clots like blood and succumbs to the memory of something unwitnessed, some other woman's desiring arms, her breasts heaving forward to his chest which you thought only you knew and spread your fingers on, guarding each special promise and his name on your tongue like a redeeming phrase, instead, the memory of another woman's careless laughter as she pulls a blouse over her head and kicks

her shoes way under the bed, another woman close to his collarbone
and resting her chin there while he presses her down, and her lips
touching the edge of his earlobe, feeling his hands knitted together under her back, binding her in a tight circle over her willing hips and his
hands dropping down to find the softest part of her, quickening his excitement so that he is sliding way down and touching her and she lifts
and shifts her whole wailing body forward and he pulls her up toward
himself and can reach her innermost part then holding and holding her
body right there where the taste of her, the feel of her, is like tomorrow
. . . his voice in another woman's ear whispering the goodness and
wordless mystery of it . . . the wanting of her . . . the feel of this. Knowing this. He pulls both her legs right round his body and she locks him
down and drops the heel of her foot in the middle of his back and he
wonders if he can wait any longer to savor this, to feel it beyond this suspended fraction of time which he knows will end, just slightly longer
than this, longer, before he touches some solid ground. Some strange
woman's solid ground, not your own. He whispers in her ear what he
will, and names her, gives a name to each part of her welcoming self,
gives her all the names you found together. Knowing this, that he could
place his beautiful slim hands somewhere else but here, breathe in that
ecstasy somewhere else but here, entangle his breathing with somebody
else's breathing but not this breathing and this body, and be able to look
shamelessly into this stranger's eyes when his hips are full and satisfied,
collapse those hips and his full weight between another woman's raised
knees, the thought of all this is too much like a slow death and the
tongue grows heavy as lead, and the knocking way up in the roof of the
mouth will not stop till something else gives in, some window opens or
the stars all fall from the sky. And another name has to be found for that
lingering ache where the desire used to be and your eyes are just open
with nothing but dismay, then the blood starts pumping from your

heels rising up to your head louder than anything and deaf with the endless sorrow of it, deaf to all the world but the blood flowing upward and downward and separating your core, the gist of you, strand after strand, and it is no longer you lying there under this body but some other body, and you wonder at the purpose of being alive and so unchosen, so unspecial, so forgotten, so dead, and if you are so dead why are you breathing on and on in this insatiable manner, unable to command your body to stop breathing because yes, you know how to do that, to hold your breath tight like a fist, instead everything is beating loudly just to remind you how truly alive you are, how trapped in all the minute details of living, your knees bending and folding away, your elbow breaking, and your mind kneading its memories.

It would have been better to have died sooner, and been buried in that fine sand she had found and held, which she could still feel vanishing between her fingers.

Who was this other woman, and when?

n i n e t e e n

How did Deliwe know the things she did not know about Fumbatha, the secret things which no one tells no one but someone tells someone only because they think this someone is not anyone any longer but themselves.

Fumbatha had never told her that his father was hanged together with sixteen others in 1896. He definitely never told her that because how could she forget a thing like that. It was Deliwe who let her know about it, saying to her with raised eyebrows that "A man whose father was hanged by a white man has a lot of pride. He must be treated with care." Phephelaphi asked her about which man and which hanging tree and which seventeen. It interested her to know how Deliwe knew what she, Phephelaphi, who slept with Fumbatha every night did not know, and when had Deliwe started knowing the secrets in the body of Fumbatha.

She did not have to ask because Deliwe was eager to tell her. Deliwe was one of those women who has no fear in watching another woman turn to ashes. She told, about each detail of her life with Fumbatha, she, the older one, telling the younger, not knowing that her telling was the entire separation of life and death, that the life of the young one had ended. Phephelaphi had to ask, to confirm that this was not just a fine punishment for all her wrongs but that indeed this was nothing but truth, so she asked Deliwe if she knew anything about the cream scar shaped like a mountain on Fumbatha's skin, and where was it. Deliwe knew. There was no knowing where it was without pulling his trousers down and climbing those hills with him, that mountain with ragged plateaus, so Phephelaphi let Deliwe go on, about the whispering after they lay down spent, about hanged men disappearing in trees. She wondered why Fumbatha had rescued her from the Umguza River without loving her enough to tell her this truest thing, then all their days together seemed to wilt into nothing, to become shapeless, since she knew nothing about him and he was only waiting for a fifty-year-old love who would understand better than she anything he had to say to someone, not anybody, Deliwe, a woman who knew how to make any man forget his grief. Phephelaphi did not have to ask what Deliwe had whispered back. She had whispered all the things Phephelaphi had told her and that is how he knew.

Deliwe to whom everything was fast paced and familiar knew nothing of birds with broken wings because she had watched a car reverse into her own body and survived. She had scorpions in her eyes and called upon them whenever she needed them. To her, Phephelaphi was a young girl who could find another love without even leaving Sidojiwe E2.

After all, Fumbatha was the one who had entered Deliwe's doorway and blocked the departing sun and remained there till she put her arms around him. He was the one who had asked for a sip of whatever liquid she could bring carried on the nail of her smallest finger. She had dipped her hand in the sweetest liquid she could find and brought it to him. On that same night she knew the exact year his father had died and he had been born. It had been easy.

Deliwe forgot that she had closed the door quickly and efficiently as soon as Fumbatha's foot was past the doorway, or that between each of his words she had raised her elbows high as though there was a burden she had to lift and instead searched with her fingers for the tightest knot that she could find, let it loose, and pulled down her own red scarf from her head. She leaned against the closed door and kept the door down as though it had a will of its own and would open wide and invite him to change his mind.

Deliwe had waited with her arms held tightly in front of her, diagonally across each other, her hands curled over each shoulder. With the red scarf hanging down like a long silky rope from her left shoulder to her feet, she slid just one foot out, her left, and rested her entire sole carelessly above the top of the shoe, crushing the black leather down. When Fumbatha knelt down, he had already seen the inside curve of her foot, soft, and heard her offer a melody which asked what kind of dance was a fox-trot since everyone at Stanley Dance Hall, in Makokoba, was whispering about it. And all good things considered, what kind of a dance was a Two-by-Two, and did anyone know if it was sweeter than rain, and if someone knew that then that someone also had to tell if a dove ever could hatch its young by the light of the moon. Deliwe slid all the way down the door and let her scarf fall to the floor where she intended it to lie for the entire night while all her four candles melted the darkness down. With her head bare, with her shining black hair exposed, Fumbatha knew that the scorpions had already left Deliwe's eyes. He gathered her like spilling water, as though parts of Deliwe would vanish before he made up his mind, or he had enough time to recall the last true thing she had said.

Deliwe left Phephelaphi's door ajar, as the policeman had done in her own house. Deliwe missed the light that first flickered in Phephelaphi's eyes when she entered the room and died instantly when she departed.

Phephelaphi left the door open and decided Fumbatha would close it when he returned from wherever, maybe he was already waiting for Deliwe at her house at the end of Sidojiwe E2. Phephelaphi rose from the edge of the bed only to do one thing, to check inside all the pockets of his worn-out leather jacket and find, if it was true, the handmade bamboo flute which Deliwe claimed she had given to Fumbatha. A token which Fumbatha had accepted. She searched with the rapid ease she had watched Deliwe muster on that first afternoon she had followed her to her house like a dog. That was the last thing she had to confirm and if she did not find it none of this would be true at all and she would be all right, she could lie back down on the bed and everything would calm down to a steady tone that she could survive. Everything would halt like train engines while she was still all right, her breath steady and able. She found the flute quickly and easily, a tiny flute, and she held it close to her lips with trembling hands to hear just one note rise clearly out of it. She brought her lips to it but her breath could not follow the movement of her lips, so she laid it down beside her, on the bed, because everything was too burdensome for her. She fell back on the bed and rested her head down.

Where was he? He had left the milk bottle open while the flies buzzed all over it. He left the newspaper on the floor with all the pages mixed together. He left his belt over there by the bench, its metal buckle touching the ground. When, if ever, would she pick the broom and scrape the cobwebs stretching in the four corners underneath the bench. He left her sitting here with empty arms and Deliwe waltzing right in as though she had been in this room before, knowing exactly where Phephelaphi was seated and which words to say before turning back, her heels clicking, leaving her door ajar.

When he walked back into the room Fumbatha saw her holding the flute and Phephelaphi asked him why the flute, why Deliwe, why the secret of his father.

"You killed our child?" he asked, finally. His eyebrows raised mockingly, telling her without words that nothing could be more important than that and why was she wasting the last light of the evening on anything less important than her betrayal.

"Not Deliwe. Were you with Deliwe? She has been here telling me some strange news. Do you know anything about it, Fumbatha?"

Her voice was fading. It was pleading. He could hear her but he had ceased to care. Instead a cloud burst and suddenly he had two heads. He walked toward her and pointed his furrowed face down at her. He watched her as though they had just met. He did not know her. She kept her eyes focused on his and tried to lead him back to where they began, to the Umguza River where they had both seen the sun leap out of the water. She carried the memory of this in her eyes. She pleaded against this constricted face she knew nothing about with its promise of a fierce storm. He picked the flute from the bed and threw it across the room. It hit the wall and made one hard sound like breaking bone, then fell to the floor. She recalled the stone which had been thrust through the window, and her fear and isolation. This fracture and splinter was much more frightening because in it he had rejected both of them. The flute fell to the floor in two halves. A static crackling which had nothing in it but death and breaking bone. The room was quiet except for his arms waiting. He turned back to her. She heard every word.

"You are nothing. Now I know a young girl like you can be dangerous. How did you do it? Did you go back to your mother's friend, that Zandile, where you had been staying when I met you, on number eight L Road? The one who boiled an evil pot of cooking oil and poured that all over her husband's first wife till her skin flapped from her body and blew out like a blanket. That one. Who burned off her husband's entire arm with another pot of boiling water because of that same woman who had claimed him first. I know that Zandile, do you think I do not know all about her and the fact that Boyidi remains with her only to save his own life? I know everything about your mother too. Your mother, Getrude. She was killed by her lover, a white policeman who shot at her when he found her talking to another man at her door when he called on her after midnight. The white policeman who then took it upon himself to bury her for you because he knew all about it since he was there. Perhaps she had killed his child too though I do not think he would have cared, but he cared enough about her meeting someone else. Did he not? He shot and buried her calmly too. I saved your life. Zandile would have killed you by now because she destroys anything that Boyidi looks at and admires. She would have killed you for sure. Did you think she would keep you alive forever? Now you have killed my child without telling me about it? Where did you bury my child?"

Phephelaphi lay still with her teeth chattering because every word he said pierced her like a spear. He shattered her entire core and she became nothing, even more than she ever thought possible. She could never gaze at a star or walk again or lift her arms to clear cobwebs from her path, anything which required the swing of her arm or her feet rising was now impossible for her. Her legs felt light, more hollow than bamboo, weightless, and she was floating like a lone feather, suspended between each of his cutting words. She died like a spark of flame. Her eyes blind and stinging not with tears but with the throbbing in her head, the despair, she could taste metal or glass or something like that which kept sliding in and out and over her tongue, tiny rough splinters cutting up her tongue, and her whole body was still because if she hoisted herself up to see what he was saying whatever was left of her true self would vanish, and in any case a sound was coming toward her like a tree falling but she was too weak to move her body away from the jutting branches tearing her face away, blinding her. She was uprooted but where would she find new ground? In the midst of this dream she was no longer living and Fumbatha was not there at all in front of her but his voice was following her, accusing her, and taking Boyidi's hands and placing them all over her body. Boyidi did not mind this at all. He was a man who loved moonlight and whatever lay beneath it, fireflies, crawling insects, a woman caught in a single ribbon of light. Phephelaphi remained still and did not move and Fumbatha stood aside while Boyidi did with her whatever he wished. She did not resist. Zandile pretended it did not matter and yet she planned to destroy her with whatever hot liquid she could find. Planned, that was all. She could do nothing more than make a plan. Zandile could never kill her because she was her own true mother and knew it. She had given her over to Getrude to keep. Zandile could not kill her own child to whom she had given birth and nearly died while doing it because this child refused to come out on its own. The doctor had to take a knife and slice Zandile down the middle, and pull the child out. Zandile did not want either this child who refused to be born or the bold magnificent scar left falling below her navel which ruined the mood of her every subsequent encounter with each man. A child was an agony then, with absolutely no man she could point to and share the burden with. She could not keep this child. The city was beckoning and she had just knocked on its large waiting door. She was determined to find its flamboyant edges, its color and light, and above all else if she could, then a man too to call her own. She needed lightness. That is what the city offered, not the burden of becoming a mother. That was a mistake and she would treat it exactly as that; a disturbance. Instead of throwing the child into a ditch and walking away as she intended to and would have successfully done, Getrude, who was her truest friend from the day both their heels hit black tar and they arrived in the city in 1920, grabbed the day-long child from her arms and nursed her, from there on, like her own. It was a light and easy surrender, she had held the pregnancy but surely that stitched-up flesh was not a birth she would choose. If Getrude wanted the child she was free to have it. A pity she could not take the stitches too. Getrude had hard times, but she wanted to prove something, perhaps. She needed a true battle between Zandile and herself, caught as she was between the city and its cold stifling stare. She did what she could with each day, with each newfound possibility. Zandile and Phephelaphi were one true flesh. So, if Phephelaphi was sleeping with Boyidi she was sleeping with the same man her own true mother was sleeping with. It was too late to tell Boyidi that he was sleeping with the child of his own woman. They went on with their true lives, the secret simmering under each closed hand, each touch, each word. By the time Boyidi met Zandile the child was grown and already belonged to Getrude. Zandile saw no need to tell him about the child, and found another point of view for her scars.

Phephelaphi felt a warm comforting liquid rise between her thighs and knew she had wet the bed, and in any case she could hear the water drip onto the floor like a tap. She did nothing else and kept silent, waiting for the words Fumbatha had spoken to stop ringing in her ears because they continued like an echo long after he had spoken, and this time she did not want to know how at all he knew, or when. Was it after he pulled her out of the river or before?

twenty

He left.

Most of all I could not bear it because I was pregnant again and could not understand how he managed to do that to me when he had stopped loving me, and knew all that he said he knew, and now, for sure I had to forget about my June Intake because there was no way they would accept me with this child growing inside me like that, and I will not. Will *not*. So I have to forget about training as a nurse altogether and what else am I to become but nothing, and he had already left me long before I knew about it, and what he had left me with, for a little while, he came back to get. My being. My woman self tearing away. My sorrowful self. No matter my need, no matter which. I will *not*. Now he has broken my stem with this child he has given me. I am

nothing. I am not here. Here is a place you can belong. I no longer belong. I am not here. And if I give him this child and let it grow, will he
come back. Will he leave Deliwe and her wondrous song. Will he rise
out of her song into mine? Nothing is mine. I will *not*. I have been
falling and falling and now it seems I have stopped falling. Stopped.
Falling. A sudden stop that leaves me breathless. I have stopped moving.
Stumbling and dropping down is better than this stillness. An absence
which means having nothing at all in my arms. All the water has dried.
There is no water in the river. A woman who is alone stands on solid
ground, on a dry riverbed. My own solid ground to match the voice
which is no longer in my arms, whispering my name.

Today I turn my arm and listen to all the silence in my bones. I hear
something beautiful. I see myself die in a storm. A storm has amazing
sounds, beautiful, like eggshells crushed between palms, only louder.
More certain. There are loud sounds and there are small sounds in a
storm. It is the small sounds which are ephemeral, thin like life, and they
make me long to die in a storm, amid its small and alluring sounds,
wrapped in those tiniest sounds; a blanket made only of petals.

A wind builds, high, as rain falls. I can hear the wind moving swiftly
between the rushing drops of rain. This is a beautiful sound. The rain
meets something solid, a sheet of air which throws the rain against a
wall: water is not heavier than air. Have you not seen all the petals fallen
from a tree during a storm? The tree is bare but the ground is beautiful.
I would like to lie beneath the petals. It is a good way to die, the ground
is soft, not hard and dry like rock.

Rain falls briefly here, but when it does, you can look up at the sky
and see clouds gather. The darkness of the clouds is the softest thing
there is. Lightning makes a beautiful sound; to die in lightning is to be
gathered in a beautiful light, more beautiful than stars. Something
opens in the sky, something beautiful which desires to be seen.

A storm begins with a strong wind, this is also the beginning of lightning. This wind sweeps all the fine soil from the ground and then hollows the earth for more—the sound is of tiny grains melting into the air. Sand floats. Sound floats. It rises further into the air and leaves the ground bare of leaves. A storm begins with a flood of grains pouring up into the sky: particles of time.

Sometimes large drops of rain fall from the sky onto the soft ground. When the first rain falls the dust rises from the ground and I can smell it and I want to fall down. I want to lie on the ground. I want to feel the rain on my tongue. Only the finest soil can rise like a fragrance, tossing tiny clouds which float high up to the knees. The rain falls in large drops. Everything is still. This rain stops suddenly and the weight of the raindrops can be felt in the unexpected silence. When I look down, the ground has numerous small holes dug into it.

The bright sun. The rain. Then the sun and rain together. The smell of the earth divine.

twenty-one

Anguish pours out like something physical and distinct. It can be held solidly like the trunk of a tree.

The door opens swiftly. There is a severe moment one wishes to retreat from because the time before, in its not-knowing, its not-tragedy, is preferable and consoling, and good. And what is good becomes whatever is calming, what restores like a torn membrane the time before.

Phephelaphi seeks her own refuge.

She is lightness, floating like flame, with flame. The flames wrap the human form, arms, knees that are herself, a woman holding her pain like a torn blanket. An enticing spectacle of a severe horror. Trapped within the warmth and the light, in a pool of glorious and unquenchable flame, not stirring, just her skin peeling off like rind as the fire buzzes unforbidden over her body in charged and illicit circles, and her hair a rank odor, the child trapped in that profanity, in that swollen body.

This side. That side. Fumbatha should have remained this side. It is his position on either side of the door which sets off the entire anguish and makes it complete. Fumbatha swings the door inward and it knocks against the iron bed frame, and he follows in innocently, whistling a tune he has picked up under the streetlights. One of those tunes which linger, is repeated without thought. Nothing lost or found. A tune without pitch or strain.

The reek of urine in the hedges. A dog dead and not buried. The smell for days, everyone murmuring that a dog has died. Now, the smell of paraffin. It is not necessary to panic or think of human flesh burning. Fumbatha walks toward the door, toward the flames, toward Phephelaphi. The fire blows over her body. That he hears instantly. The sound swallows him. Fast, fearless, astonishing.

Her body is soaked in a soft liquid. She waits. For consolation, for an opportunity as ready as wisdom. For time to yield relief. Her entire body sagged. She waits, ready to be harmed, to be freed. She seeks surrender, a death as intimate as birth. A birth as certain as love.

Putrid darkness and a memory of torture. Fire emerges from one side of the room and stands upright. Swift, manifest, and easy. She is hidden by light smooth as a rainbow. Still living. Knowing he is there in the room with her. Her body a flame searching: nothing can sanction courage but desire.

Night dissolves into surrender. Warm air from her body upon his lips, his breath slow, his arms warm. Bright light from her body. No whimpering moan or sob. No rejection of suffering. This quality of pain can only heal.

A spectrum of light finely crushed, light as a whisper.

Motionless agony. Her body reeking in a pool of flammable liquid.

The fire moves over her light as a feather, smooth like oil. She has wings. She can fly. She turns her arms over and sees them burn and raises them higher above her head, easily, tossing and turning her arms up like a burning rope. She is a bird with wings spread. She falls into a beautiful sound of something weightless rising, a blue light, a yellow light, the smell of skin burning.

Vanishing: the sound of her breathing swallowed by the flame, skin sliding off thin as a promise, her body pulling up and down, buried in the lightest water there is, not drowning, just holding her breath for a while so that she can hear the door hit the side of the bed, hear quick and hurried footsteps move into the house, see Fumbatha walk through the door, once more, toward her, without words said. Without anger, without departure. The silky light claims the distance between them.

She can whisper, before her voice turns to ash, the one true thing he will always remember. She is not sure if he can hear her fragile whisper underneath that ribbon of flame, the one true thing about their un-buried child, the one inside her body, free and weightless like herself, now, safe, now. A touch, her own genuine touch; to love her own body now, after he has loved and left it, to love her own eyebrows and her own knees, finally she has done so, embracing each part of herself with flame, deeply and specially.

A woman's solid flame, even if the ground underneath her is al-ready sliding, sliding away. And she is dying in her own storm, and can hear the wind gather over her knees, and the finest flood threatening each terraced pain, each threshold, each slope and incline, and she is underneath that flood holding her breath knowing that no matter when, no matter how, she will eventually rise into her own song. All she has to do is stop holding her breath down and let go, even though she is in a flood and buried in the most liquid breeze and will surely drown. So she does, releases her breath which she had held tightly down, a knot under her chest. As she lets go she feels nothing except her wings folding. A bird landing and closing its wings.

Falling to pieces, easy, easier than she has imagined. Much much easier than holding a man in your arms. She has died as easily as Getrude, readier than she ever could be.

She had paused for two full days, waiting, watching the arm falling slowly down from the doorway. Finding Emelda. Hearing Zandile toss a soft cushiony cry in the moonlight. Laughing at Getrude who had the foolishness to trust a man knocking on her door.

At midnight.